More praise for
ANGEL'S BIDDING

"Private detective Patricia Delaney is a '90s sleuth who uses computer databases as well as old-fashioned gumshoe savvy to solve a baffling murder in the fast-paced and intriguing ANGEL'S BIDDING. Sharon Gwyn Short's debut effort is sure to win readers to this new and lively series."
—KATHY HOGAN TROCHECK
Author of *Every Crooked Nanny*
and *To Live And Die in Dixie*

"I can think of very few debuts more promising, or more satisfying, than Sharon's (and Patricia Delaney's) in ANGEL'S BIDDING."
—WILLIAM J. REYNOLDS
Author of *The Naked Eye* and *Things Invisible*

"It is a pleasure to meet Patricia Delaney, a most unusual private eye."
—NANCY PICKARD
Author of *But I Wouldn't Want To Die There*

ANGEL'S BIDDING

Sharon Gwyn Short

FAWCETT GOLD MEDAL • NEW YORK

A Fawcett Gold Medal Book
Published by Ballantine Books
Copyright © 1994 by Sharon Gwyn Short

Library of Congress Catalog Card Number: 93-90716

ISBN 0-449-14873-4

Manufactured in the United States of America

First Edition: February 1994

To David, for believing

Our acts our angels are, or good or ill,
Our fatal shadows that walk by us still
— JOHN FLETCHER

Chapter 1

The longest hatpin had the face of an angel, and the smile of death. The angel's wings were too large for the bell-shaped body, the gaping mouth disproportionately wide for the tiny nose and eyes. The exaggerated curves of wings and mouth mocked one another and, combined, made the gold angel seem like a ghoulish jester. Patricia Delaney wondered if the angel's creator had been inept or had purposefully made the angel grotesque, perhaps weary at the thought of fulfilling yet another Victorian lady's vain request.

The other hatpins were smaller, eight inches long instead of the angel's twelve inches, and simpler in design—a square-cut ruby, set in gold with four petite diamonds in the corners, and a peacock, its proud colors faded over time.

The hatpins were lined up on Patricia's desk in a neat row—the angel in the middle, the peacock and ruby on either side. Besides being relics of another time, they all shared another characteristic. On each was skewered a message created from newspaper print.

Patricia read the messages, put them back on their carriers, then lined the hatpins up on her desk in a neat row, like brave messengers in someone's personal war.

She looked up at the woman sitting on the other side of her desk. The woman shifted in her chair uncomfortably and stared at the door. Was she having second thoughts? wondered Patricia. Perhaps she'd suddenly bolt and make a run for the door, mumbling apologies for her withdrawal along the way. Some people did, usually people with personal cases, not the business clients. Some would-be clients got as

1

far as the door, saw the sign PATRICIA DELANEY, INVESTI-
GATIVE CONSULTANT, and left without even poking a head
in to apologize for the sudden, intense need to forgo learning
the truth.

The truth, as Patricia well knew from her four years experience at investigating and thirty-four at living, is a harsh,
sometimes cruel, mistress to court. But tempting. Quite
tempting. And so the woman, Elsa Kauffman, stayed in the
chair and looked back at her.

Elsa was a thin creature who shifted and looked around
like a small animal always wary of the dangers of being
trapped. She had a narrow, pixielike face, unusually child-
like for a woman in her midforties, but any expression of
mischievousness had long ago been erased by one of worry.
Over a flowered, cotton dress she wore a tweed burgundy
suit jacket that was meant to look professional. It was too
big for her, and too hot for the sticky June day that hunkered
just outside the building. Patricia's window-unit air conditioner barely kept the heat at bay.

"This is why you really came, isn't it?" Patricia asked,
nodding toward the hatpins. She guessed the hatpin messages
were the problem uppermost in Elsa's mind, the problem that
could send Elsa bolting for the door, suddenly shy about
courting truth.

"No. Oh, no. This is—this was incidental. Yes, incidental
to the problem I came here for. Really came here for. You
see, we really need to find Andy Lawson—"

"Yes, yes," Patricia said, showing more impatience than
she intended. Elsa, she realized, would gladly repeat the
whole story of the missing real-estate agent, which she had
carefully prepared for her appointment: he hadn't come in for
several days, which was unusual; his landlady hadn't seen him;
he had no relatives nearby. One hundred thousand dollars cash
had been taken from the agency's safe. According to Elsa's
father, who owned the agency, the whole matter was too sensitive to take to the police. Kauffman Real Estate and Auctioneering was in the midst of a major development on the east

side of Cincinnati and couldn't afford any negative press. Elsa was the general manager and bookkeeper for the agency.

"Why don't you tell me what you know about these hatpins?" Patricia said.

Elsa looked at them uncomfortably, her pale blue eyes darting from the death-smiling angel to the ruby to the faded peacock. She pushed her graying brown bangs back from her perspiring brow. The rest of her hair was pulled back in a ponytail.

"They just came last week," Elsa said.

"All at once?"

"No, no, that's not what I meant. One, and then another, then the other. The angel last."

"They were mailed?"

"No. Just tucked into a white envelope, sealed. Stuck in the mailbox outside the door along with the bills and listings and things."

"So they weren't addressed at all?" Patricia asked. "Just stuck in a white envelope."

"No, not quite. I mean, I'm sorry, no, they weren't addressed like you say, in the traditional sense, anyway. But whoever sent them—or I guess left them, wouldn't you say?—whoever left them cut out the name of the agency from a newspaper ad and taped it to the front of the envelope."

Elsa stared down and played with the sash of her dress, weaving it between her fingers. She spoke so softly that Patricia leaned forward to hear her better.

"I—I think they're meant for my father specifically. I'm sure they are. His name—the person—whoever sent these things had clipped his name, too, from some ads—Father still insists on representing at least five clients even though he doesn't have the time or health really for it and—"

Elsa stopped, suddenly embarrassed at the realization that she had been rambling.

"Anyway, Father's name had been cut out and pasted above the agency name."

Patricia rubbed the white, diagonal scar on the left side of her chin and frowned down at the hatpins. Ruby, angel, pea-

cock. Ruby, angel, peacock. Would the puzzle of why someone would send poison-pen notes on hatpins make more sense
to her if she rearranged the hatpins and changed the incantation?

Perhaps, she mused, she could read them like tea leaves,
and moved them around with the tips of her fingers, not
picking them up but just sliding them. Peacock, ruby, angel.
Angel, peacock, ruby.

Patricia shook her head in mild irritation at her own
whimsy and muttered, "Nope. Doesn't make sense. Why
hatpins?"

"They were my grandmother's."

"Someone from your family, then—"

Elsa shrank back in her seat, eyes wide at the suggestion.
"No, no one from my family would do anything—I mean,
these were sold over a year ago, at auction. I—I just can't
see—" Elsa stopped suddenly.

Elsa had been hesitant and nervous since she arrived twenty
minutes early for her appointment and realized Patricia was
not quite ready for her. Patricia tried to make all her clients
feel relaxed and comfortable, and she had tried especially hard
with Elsa. Patricia considered again offering her coffee or tea.
No—that had made Elsa stutter an awkward no, thank you, as
if the idea of hospitality toward her startled her.

Patricia tried a warm smile instead and said, "Go ahead.
Just tell me what you know about these hatpins."

Elsa stretched out her hands, then folded them primly in
her lap. "I don't know much. Just that when my grandmother
died—her name was Gertrude—two weeks after her funeral—we had an auction of her things. Well, my father did.
Her house—and the things from her house. To settle the estate. But Father was an only child. . . ."

Elsa faded off, then looked sharply, defensively, at Patricia, as if she knew what Patricia must be thinking: Friedrich
Kauffman auctioned off his own mother's things right after
her funeral? Patricia did not say anything and kept smiling
encouragingly. She did not believe it was her job to judge or
analyze her clients. Leave that to the psychotherapists. Still,

it was interesting to note Elsa's expression; Patricia guessed that she must have encountered the criticism often enough from friends and relatives.

"Well, she was ninety-two. And he wanted to see it done right, out of respect for her. Father is not, as you will see—an emotional person. And we—I—kept a few things." Elsa shook her head as if to clear it. "Anyway. I remember seeing them at the auction and I thought—I thought they were pretty."

"You hadn't seen them before?"

"No—I—" Elsa stopped and stared down at the hatpins. A shadow of expression, of something too painful to fully remember passed over her face.

Elsa cleared her throat and looked up at Patricia. "No, I hadn't. I guess she wore them in Germany, and she came here with Father just before the Second World War. Grandmother always said she loved beautiful things as a girl. My grandfather was a jeweler and clockmaker, so he gave her many beautiful jewels, although the hatpins had been her mother's, my father told me. He remembered them when he saw them at the auction. But after the first war came hard times, and then my grandfather died, and when trouble started up again, Grandmother brought my father and came here to live with her brother. She always said after all that she just didn't feel like wearing beautiful things. And she didn't. She was always plainly dressed. No hats."

"And so, no hatpins for you to recall. But you figure she brought them with her," Patricia said.

Elsa nodded. "Yes. With all her other jewels. I wore them—I wore them playing dress-up. As a girl."

"But you don't remember the hatpins."

Elsa looked at the hatpins, then quickly away, as if there were something shameful in her inability to remember them. "No, I don't."

"And you can attach no significance to them other than that you believe they belonged to your grandmother all this time, since they were among her possessions at the auction of her estate."

"That's right."

Patricia jotted down a few notes, then said, "It would help if you knew who purchased the hatpins."

"Oh, yes. I know that. Rosie's Attic. It's an antique shop. I remember the name because it's so—so romantic. The owner bought the hatpins, just the hatpins that day."

"Do you remember the owner's name?" Patricia asked.

"No. But it's in here." Elsa hefted an oversized, man's-style, hard-sided briefcase onto her lap, clicked it open, and pulled out a file and placed it on Patricia's desk next to the hatpins. "I keep precise records of all our auctions, all our real-estate transactions going at least ten years back. Taxes, you know. The government is very watchful of small business."

"Of course," Patricia said. Patricia was intrigued by how her client's nervousness abruptly disappeared, replaced by confident efficiency when it came to keeping business records.

"I'll just make a copy of this—"

"This is a copy. Your copy."

Patricia took a deep breath and then slowly released it. Elsa's efficiency convinced her that she had come about the hatpins and their notes as much as about the missing agent, even if she wanted to deny it.

"Fine," Patricia said. "I'll start by talking with the antique-shop owner. And I need to know who might want to frighten or threaten your father. You mentioned a business partner earlier, for starters."

Elsa's pale eyes widened at the question. She rocked back in her chair as if she had been physically repulsed by it. "My—my father doesn't have any enemies," Elsa said, then paused to clear her throat. "He is a well-respected business-man in real estate. I'm sure you've heard of him before now. He built the Eagle Rise development and he's involved in another development project now. He's well respected. He doesn't have enemies."

Patricia tossed the pad and pencil back on her desk and picked up the angel-head hatpin. She held it up for a minute for Elsa to observe, then put it down with the ruby and peacock.

"Someone went to a lot of effort to get just the right hatpin and message together, and get them to your father in a way that is going to make it very hard to trace where they came from—no postmark, no handwriting," Patricia said, keeping her voice as even as she could. "My guess is that these all add up to a message your father is supposed to understand—and be frightened of. So he's got at least one enemy somewhere in this world. It's no insult; we all do, Ms. Kauffman. At least one."

Patricia paused and studied Elsa Kauffman. Perhaps this petite woman didn't have even one enemy. She looked scared, vulnerable, a tiny creature quivering with the desire to duck back into a dark, safe spot in her private woods. It was possible that someone like this had remained uninvolved in the world enough to avoid having even one enemy.

But no. Elsa was here, in Patricia's office, so she hadn't completely withdrawn from life. If only because there are people in the world who despise fear in others because it reminds them of their own vulnerabilities, Elsa would have enemies. Just sensing the unnamed fear in Elsa, as palpable as a scent, would make those people hate her, make them want to wipe her, and thus the fear, out. Patricia had a theory that that sort of unfortunate chemistry accounted for more than a few muggings each year.

Elsa smiled tentatively. "I'm sorry I'm not much help on this. But I honestly can't think of any enemies of my father's."

"How about the missing agent"—Patricia ruffled through the papers and notes Elsa had brought about him—"Andy Lawson?"

"No—oh no, not Andy. My father always says that Andy is like the son to him he never had."

And yet, thought Patricia, Elsa, and apparently her father, were so certain that Andy's disappearance meant he'd taken the $100,000.

Patricia decided against pointing that out and asked, "You're an only child?" It wasn't really pertinent to the investigation, but Patricia was curious. Domineering father, maybe the mother died young, resulting in an only daughter who grows up to be too devoted to her father and too timid with everyone else.

"No, I have a sister and brother," Elsa said. "I guess my brother didn't quite turn out the way he wanted—the way my father wanted, that is. My brother likes himself just fine. Anyway he—my father, that is—he is quite upset that Andy—and—and the money from the safe are missing. That is why he told me to find a private investigator."

Patricia glanced at the personal computer on her desk. So much for guesses. That's why she relied on research on computer databases, interviews, the occasional tailing, and other investigative tools.

She gestured at the hatpins. "What does your father say about these?"

Elsa stared into her lap and began playing with the sashes of her dress. "He doesn't."

"He has no opinion at all?"

"No. He doesn't—he doesn't even know they arrived." Elsa looked up quickly with pleading eyes. "He has so much on his mind lately—Andy—the development. I didn't want to trouble him. And—and he would just say they are nothing—silly anyway."

"How can you be sure of that?"

Elsa's pale eyes suddenly became icy. "I've worked for my father for over twenty years. He would say they are silliness."

"But you think they are more than just silliness. A real threat."

"Yes."

"Why?"

Elsa stared at the hatpins, frowning, as if they entranced her, even though—perhaps because—she remembered nothing about them.

"I don't know," she said. "I just do. If you could be so kind as to bill me individually—personally, for looking into them. And if you could refrain from mentioning them to my father for now, until you find out more—''

"Fine, then, to summarize—" Patricia looked down at her notepad. "I'll look first into Andy Lawson's disappearance. I can't assume he took the money, but he is a good enough place to start. I'll talk to the antique-shop owner about the hatpins. When I find out what he has to say about them, I'll let you know.''

"That sounds fine.''

"You'll have to decide then if you want me to talk about them with your father. I think that will be necessary for establishing why he might be getting them. Meanwhile, I'll find your agent and your money. Sound okay?''

Patricia made a few more notes as she waited for Elsa's response. When she didn't get one, she looked back up at her. Elsa was still staring at the hatpins.

"Elsa? Does that sound okay?" Patricia urged.

Elsa looked up at Patricia. She smiled thinly, the smile of a sick or injured person bravely denying the pain.

"Yes, fine. I'll look forward to hearing from you.'' She stood up and so did Patricia. The women exchanged handshakes—Patricia's grasp firm and quick, Elsa's hand moist and yielding.

"Thank you, I'll be in touch,'' Patricia said.

Elsa turned and started for the door.

"Oh—one last question. Your office is in Blue Ash?'' Patricia asked.

"Yes.'' Blue Ash was a suburb north of Cincinnati.

"And you live there, too?''

"Yes.''

Patricia smiled. Most of her clients were people from the suburbs on the north and east sides of Cincinnati—people who wanted to check out a spouse or employee or partner, but discreetly. She realized wryly that, for most of her clients, hiring an investigative consultant in a suburb was more appealing than hiring a private eye in the city. But Elsa wasn't like most of her clients.

"I went to school here once, to Alliston College,'' Elsa

offered suddenly. She stared at the window at the back of Patricia's office as if she could see the college on the hill, even though the only view the window afforded was of a boarded-up corner gas station.

"Chemistry. I studied chemistry and physics there for three years before I went to work in the family business." She shook her head, then smiled thinly. "But that was a while ago. Anyway, thanks again."

Patricia nodded. "I'll be in touch."

After Elsa left, Patricia got up, shrugged off her black, lightweight jacket, and hung it on the small coatrack next to her navy-blue and tan jackets. They were her only three jackets. She kept them at the office and wore them over whatever she happened to be wearing when clients showed up. If it matched, fine; if not, fine.

That day she had on a bright yellow dress with black polka dots, short-sleeved and straight cut, and black pumps, so it had worked out. There was satisfaction in that for Patricia. She liked it when things worked out.

She went over to the window air conditioner, fiddled with the controls, then gave it a good smack. The unit moaned and kept emitting tepid air. Patricia switched the unit from cool to fan and opened the window. The heavy smell of greasy sugar from the donut shop below coated the sticky June air and drifted in the window.

Patricia went back to her desk, stretched her tall, statuesque frame, then sat back down. She flicked on the computer, intending to write up the notes from Elsa Kauffman's visit.

But the hatpins, still out on her desk, and a sense of restlessness after Elsa's visit, distracted her. She reread the notes skewered on each hatpin: the angel carried the message *Do you know who was watching?*; the ruby offered, *I remember*; the peacock's message could have been cut from a Sunday-school primer, *Pride before a fall*.

Patricia returned to the angel's-head hatpin and twirled it between her fingers, watching the head with its mawkish grin twirl to the right, then the left. There was something about the case that bothered her already. It wasn't just the unusual request of tracking the sender of the hatpins and threatening notes—a little change from checking out errant spouses and employees, or doing background checks on potential partners (business and otherwise) was fine with her. It was the nearly palpable fear that Elsa had exuded. Was Elsa really just a person who walked in fear generally, or had her fear been provoked by the hatpins?

Patricia shook her head, wiped the back of her hand across her brow, and ran her fingers through her nearly black, short, curly hair. She looked at the framed photograph of a waterfall on the wall across from her, one of several photos she had used to decorate her office. The waterfall photo, published in a nature magazine the year before, was one of her best efforts from her modestly successful avocation as an amateur photographer.

Patricia tried to focus on the image of the waterfall and return to the sense of centeredness that she had surely felt when she had taken the photo. She could not. The images of the hatpins kept imposing themselves on her mind.

Suddenly she swept the hatpins into her lap drawer, deciding to find a box for them later. Putting her hands over her eyes, she took several deep breaths, focusing on the slow in and out of her breathing.

But still the hatpins, even tucked out of sight in her lap drawer, kept intruding on her thoughts.

Patricia pushed back from her desk and looked over her notes on the computer screen. She'd find Andy and the missing money. And she'd try to find who was sending the hatpins and the messages, if that was what Elsa really wanted her to do. But whatever fear was driving the woman—she wasn't getting wrapped up in that. Patricia had tried to be an angel of mercy once before, and so she knew sometimes that meant becoming a messenger of doom. She was not prepared for either role again.

Chapter 2

After the second-to-last set of Jay Bell and the Queen River Band, the patrons at Dean's Tavern were fired up, restless, ready for one more round of drinks. Patricia thought the last set had been the night's most mediocre, but the crowd had not seemed to notice or care. The people had risen from their chairs, clapping and clamoring, glad for one last set before the weary, dark drive home brought the realization that the next day's demands were so close.

Patricia hopped up onto an empty bar stool and surveyed the little groups and couples gathered around the crude wooden tables. Squinting through the smoky, dim light, she smiled as she watched Jay working the crowd, pausing at each table to chat and take requests. The patrons were mostly of the young, affluent, rising-corporate-star set, at least on Tuesday nights, from the suburbs north and east of Cincinnati, out for a night in a nice, "real" country town. They weren't really escaping the suburbs, Patricia would have regretted to tell them if she'd gone in for mixing between sets—Alliston was just a slightly remote satellite east of the big city.

But then Patricia Delaney had long understood and been intrigued by the fact that nothing is entirely what it seems. Jay was really Jacobus Bellosi—but as he said, what kind of name was that for a classic rock band? Jay, an attorney bored by his position in a large law firm, had two passions: his band and his boat, *Queen of the River*, after which his band was named. The boat itself was christened after Cincinnati's nickname, the Queen City, and the fact that Cincinnati was on the curving banks of the Ohio River. Jay was the lead singer and guitar player. Jasmine Domini, sitting at a table with her husband and parents-in-law, was a veterinarian by day and singer and bass guitar player by night. Gary Johnson, keyboardist, sat silently with Jasmine's group. An accountant by day, he always came alone and kept quiet on most topics, including his reasons for needing a Tuesday-night escape into musical mini-stardom.

That left Patricia. She played drums, and occasionally the fiddle, with the band on its weekly Tuesday-night appearance at Dean's. She never really cared what the band played. It was enough for her to get lost in the beat of her drums, to know nothing but herself and the rhythm as one, part of a musical whole.

"You look like you could use a drink, lady."

Patricia swiveled away from the crowd to face the bar and looked up into the laughing blue eyes of Dean O'Reilly, owner of the bar. She smiled. He smiled back and kept polishing a glass.

"You're right. The usual."

Dean nodded. He gave the glass a final swipe, then prepared her favorite drink, iced coffee with a shot of bourbon. On Tuesday nights he kept a pitcher of iced coffee for her in the mini-refrigerator beneath the bar, a fact that pleased Patricia. Dean sat the glass in front of her, then watched her quickly pick it up and take a thirsty swallow.

"Long set?" he said, after she put the glass back down on the countertop and wiped her mouth with the back of her hand.

"Long day."

Dean leaned across the bar and peered into her eyes. "Yeah. Your usually brilliant green eyes are red. It's from sitting too long in front of that little gray box."

Patricia rolled her eyes, nevertheless enjoying the familiar banter. "Give me a break. It's this smoke-filled tavern. And show a little respect for my computer, okay?"

Dean threw up his hands in mock surrender. "Sure. God

knows what you might be able to dig up on me with that thing.''

Patricia arched an eyebrow. ''You have something to hide?''

Dean grinned. ''Of course. So did you learn anything, staring in that little gray box of yours, cooped up in your office all day? Shades drawn, I bet.''

''Geez, you make me sound like a fungus.'' Patricia took another sip of the coffee, letting the cool liquid puddle on her tongue for a moment before swallowing. ''As a matter of fact, I learned a lot of fascinating things today. Like about hatpins.''

''Hatpins?'

''Yeah, you know, these long pins ladies used to use to keep their hats in place. Sort of pinned their hats to their hair. Especially popular in the Victorian era. Came in all sorts of designs—quite expensive, some of them. You know, hatpins.''

''You mean, you didn't already know all that about hat-pins?'' Dean liked to tease Patricia.

''Just proves the little gray box's worth, don't you think? Didn't know, either, that it's still in the law books in Chicago that it's illegal to carry a hidden hatpin. It's considered a concealed weapon. Women used to use them for self-defense.''

''Can a hatpin do that much damage?''

Patricia shrugged. ''In the right hands, I guess, or the law wouldn't have been necessary. Standard hatpins are either eight inches or twelve inches long. That's long enough, and a hatpin is sharp enough to cause serious damage—or death— if it pierces a vital organ.''

''Maybe you ought to pack a hatpin. Self-protection. Never needs reloading.''

''Mmm. Except the only hat I wear is an occasional base-ball cap. Hatpins wouldn't quite do.''

''I don't know, you'd look kind of cute in one of those old-fashioned big hats. . . .''

Patricia wrinkled her nose. "Please. I never look cute. It's against my morals."

Dean grinned at that, to show he knew better, and Patricia ignored him by concentrating on her iced coffee and bourbon. Dean and Patricia had met the first night she'd played with the Queen River Band, during the break after the first set. That had been four months ago. They quickly became friends, their relationship occasionally edging toward more, but always, for now, retreating to the safety and reliability of friendship. Patricia had her reasons for wanting to keep it that way, at least for a while. She'd never asked Dean what he preferred.

"Still, you know what the little gray box didn't tell me about hatpins?" Patricia asked.

"I'm fascinated. What?"

"Why someone would send threatening notes to someone else on hatpins. Kind of like poison-pen shish kebabs."

Dean picked up another glass and started polishing it. "Maybe it symbolizes something the person getting the notes is supposed to understand."

"I got that far. Like what?"

"Like maybe they're supposed to stick it?"

Patricia groaned, and then laughed out loud. Dean always managed to make her laugh, even with a bad joke. It was one reason she liked him so much.

Dean went off to serve another customer. For a few minutes Patricia nursed her drink, listening to the sounds of the bar around her—murmuring voices, clinking glass and china, a phone ringing in the back, the bang of the kitchen door.

"Phone's for you."

Patricia looked up and saw Jeanne standing behind the bar. Jeanne worked a few nights a week at Dean's Tavern. All that Patricia knew about her was that she was also an Alliston College student who always seemed depressed.

"For me?"

"Yeah, unless you're a double for Patricia Delaney."

"Not lately. Who is it? Did they say?"

Jeanne shrugged. "I didn't take a message. I just said

yeah, you were here, I'd get you. Woman, though. Sounded long distance."

"Right. Keep an eye out for me, will you, for the time for the next set?" Patricia said, then realized it was pointless to ask Jeanne to keep her mind focused that completely. "Never mind, just let Jay know where I am."

Patricia went behind the bar, then walked down a little hall, past the kitchen doors and the rest rooms, to Dean's cramped office, originally a luxuriously large storage closet.

The door was ajar, and she went in. On one of the stacks of paper on the desk lay the receiver to the phone. Patricia braced herself to tolerate the clutter, then picked up the receiver.

"Hello?" she said tentatively. For a crazy half second she wondered if Elsa Kauffman had somehow tracked her down here, and the thought sent a shot of foreboding through her.

Then the familiar voice, desperation overcoated with cheeriness, came through the static on the line. "Patty-cakes? It's me!"

Patricia closed her eyes, inwardly grimacing at the childhood nickname. "Maureen," she said softly. The only shock was in hearing the voice again this soon after the last plea for help. Normally the pleas, for a sympathetic shoulder or cash, were spaced a year or so apart. The last one, six months ago, had been for cash.

"C'mon, little sister," Maureen said, laughing nervously. Her laugh gave way to a smoker's hack. "You don't sound thrilled to hear from me."

"Just surprised, that's all. Normally it's a little longer between your calls. How did you track me down here?"

"You mentioned in your letter that you were playing drums with a band, and the place. Wouldn't Dad be thrilled to hear what his former little music star is doing?" Maureen laughed again.

Her letter. Patricia wrote Maureen lots of letters, more than she meant to. In a letter she could pretend she was talking to the old Maureen of years before. Sometimes Maureen even wrote back, in a cheerful, lighthearted tone that made it seem really believable. The pretense only fell apart whenever they talked on the phone or saw each other. It had been five years since they'd seen each other.

Patricia sighed at again picking up the old lines, the old defense patterns. "I was never a star, Maureen, not even to Dad. Just a violin student who didn't get too far. And as it turns out, he thought it was neat that I'm playing drums with a band. At least, as he put it, it's something musical. Speaking of which, you're lucky you caught me on a break between sets."

"I get it; I'll hurry up. I tried your office and home and you weren't at either place, and something's come up."

"You could have left a message."

"Yeah. But I need a favor. I can't ask a machine for a favor."

"Uh-huh."

"C'mon, Patricia, don't sound like that. It's not money, or problems this time. In fact, things are going better than ever for me now—"

"And you're calling me? Should I get the bar to break out the champagne? Maureen Lucinda Delaney Walsh Smith Cray Stophono did I get all that right? finally gets her shit together."

"I thought you'd be happy for me."

"I haven't heard anything concrete yet. I have heard you say umpteen times that things are going better for you."

"They are this time. I've met this man, Rick—"

"Oh, Sweet St. Peter."

"No, you'd like Rick. He's not—he's not like the others."

Patricia stared up at the ceiling. The others had been ex-cons, executives, bums, salesmen, a doctor, Baker, butcher, candlestick maker. Who could keep track? They all had one thing in common—they were all mean, abusive, and controlling, leaving Maureen with an occasional bruise and a perpetually broken heart. Maureen was addicted to the type, and the addiction had kept her from ever keeping a nice guy, a nice job, a nice place to live, a nice anything for very long. The only thing steady in her life, besides pain, was her daughter, Lucy.

"So are you calling to tell me wedding bells are once again on the horizon for you?"

"Maybe . . . nothing that serious, yet. But I don't want to blow it with Rick. He's got his own business, lots of money. He's rich, Patty."

"So what do you want from me, Maureen, a character witness? I hereby testify my sister would make a great rich man's wife."

"Cut it out, Patty-cakes. This is serious. Look, he's asked me to come with him to his lodge in the mountains for a few weeks. Talk things over, you know?"

"Great."

"Yeah, but there's Lucy."

"What about her?"

"I can't exactly take her with me."

"Maureen, she's what, sixteen now? Just leave her at home."

Maureen coughed. "I—I'm kind of worried about her, Patty. Her friends—aren't the greatest. I think they're into drugs and—who knows what else. She's talking about not going to college—she's talking about going off to New York with her guitar and some no-talent friends to form a punk band."

Patricia grinned. "Music has always run strong in our family."

"I could send her to a state school," Maureen continued, as if she hadn't heard Patricia's comment at all. "But Rick, with his money, she could go to a private school. . . . Look, for both Lucy's and my sake I need to make this a success with Rick. He and I need some time. I can't keep worrying about Lucy. . . ."

"So?" Whatever Maureen said, her desires for success with Rick were wrapped around her own needs, not Lucy's.

"So I thought she could come stay with you. I've already talked with her about it, and she said yeah, she'd be willing to spend a few weeks with Auntie Patty. . . ."

Patricia bolted up in the chair. "Sweet St. Peter, Maureen! Who do you think I am, Mother Goose? I've got a business to run, a bunch of other stuff going on in my life. . . . Why don't you call Mom and Dad? Or Sean? Or Kelly, or Ryan?" But Patricia knew the answer to that. Their parents would agree to taking Lucy. Their brothers and sister . . . they had learned better than to rescue Maureen, long ago. Patricia hadn't, but she had reasons they didn't know and probably wouldn't understand.

"You know I can't ask any of them for anything."

"They'd all still love to hear from you. Especially Mom and Dad. How long has it been—"

"Okay, okay. I don't need lectures, I need a place for Lucy for a few weeks."

Patricia heard a knock at the door. She opened it. Jay stood in the doorway, pointing at his watch and looking worried. Patricia nodded, held up a finger to indicate just a moment more, and pushed the door shut with her foot.

"Okay, Maureen, I'd love to stay and argue with you, but I've got to get back to the band. Lucy can come and stay with me—just for a few weeks—and tell her she'd better like sandwiches, preferably ones she makes herself. I'm not Betty Crocker, either."

Patricia could almost hear Maureen smiling through the phone. Why was it, she thought, that she felt certain that Maureen had somehow managed to time the call so she'd catch her on a break, when she wouldn't have time to figure out a way to say no to her? But then she'd never said no to Maureen's requests before.

"That's great, Patty, that's great! I knew I could count on you. Lucy'll be coming in on the Greyhound from Detroit next Thursday, two forty-five, at the Cincinnati station—"

"You already bought her ticket?" Patricia opened the desk drawer to find a scrap of paper and a pen to write down the details. "You mean you—"

"Thanks, Patty!"

The line went dead. Patricia looked for a moment at the phone receiver, then put it down, laughing. Of course Maureen had already bought the ticket. Maureen had known Auntie Patty wouldn't be able to deny her request, no matter how sudden or inconvenient.

Patricia sifted through the mess in Dean's drawer, pushing aside the nine-millimeter semiautomatic he casually kept among the paper clips and rubber bands and assorted junk. For protection, he'd told her once, though how he'd get back here and find the gun in this mess in the heat of a robbery was beyond her. Patricia smiled. Maybe Dean would be better off with a hatpin in his pocket. Patricia found a blank scrap of notepaper and a pen and wrote down Lucy's arrival time, then folded the slip neatly and put it in her jean's back pocket.

Patricia went back up to the bar. Jay was eyeing her nervously from the miniature stage, but she needed to talk to Jeanne first.

"Jeanne, the woman who called me. How many times did she call tonight?"

Jeanne stared off, as if she hadn't even heard the question. Then she looked back slowly at Patricia. "Twice."

"What did she say the first time?"

"That she wanted to talk to you, it was important. I told her you were busy. She said she knew you played in a band and asked when would the next break be."

"And you told her?"

"Yeah. Shouldn't I have?" Jeanne asked defensively.

"It's okay, Jeanne. Just curious. Thanks."

Patricia went to her drums, settled down on the stool, picked up her sticks, ready to provide a backbeat for the final set of songs. As the first song started up it crossed her mind that her sister, even with her veneer of toughness, was a lot like Elsa Kauffman.

Chapter 3

Patricia's office occupied the smallest suite on the second floor of a two-story building in an office and shopping park called, optimistically, Prosperity Plaza. In the four years she had been in the office working independently, she had built her business so that she relied more on referrals from satisfied customers than from her previous employer, Adam's Security and Investigations, in downtown Cincinnati. Three years at Adam's had taught her investigative skills and enabled her to get her license, but she had known almost immediately that she needed to work independently. She began saving for her solo venture after her third week at Adam's.

Now Patricia sat at her desk, putting the finishing touches on a preliminary report on Andy Lawson. Elsa had called her the evening before, saying that her father wanted a progress report. Elsa had made the request sound like a summons.

After hearing her report, Patricia thought Friedrich Kauffman would wish he had employed her to review Andy's background before he'd hired him. With Andy's current address and social security number, courtesy of Elsa, Patricia had unearthed his unsavory past by searching through several databases on her computer, some public domain, some reserved only for licensed private investigators. The computer was an information-age tool that Patricia, and a growing number of her colleagues, relied on as an inevitable part of the modern investigator's tool kit.

Andy had a history of bad-check writing; skipped rent on two past landlords; had a terrible credit rating; and was guilty

21

of receiving stolen goods, numerous automotive violations, and a fraud scam in his hometown, Morris, Utah. He moved quickly from place to place; she found twelve addresses for him in three states in the last three years. He had never been married and owned no property. His longest on the job stint had been with the Kauffmans, for the past six months. Patricia had also contacted a detective in Utah through a computerized electronic bulletin board reserved only for licensed private investigators. The Utah investigator was planning to get back to her soon with a thorough list of relatives and friends, culled from Andy's hometown newspaper, which was not yet available on a computer database.

Patricia sent her report to the printer, stood up from her desk, and stretched, enjoying the satisfaction of a job thoroughly done, and surveyed her office with pleasure.

In the four years that she'd been in the office, she'd slowly improved its appearance. She had stripped the dull green wallpaper and painted the walls a subtle buff; put up prints of her best photographs; replaced the dirty white drapes with sky-blue mini-blinds and a valance; and put two large, healthy ficus trees on either side of the window. Her desk, second-hand from a used-office-supply warehouse, faced the front door. On her desk she kept a vase filled each week with fresh flowers. Her chair and the matching visitors' chairs were new. Against a side wall she had set up a small table with a coffee service for her clients. She still didn't like the carpet, a yellow, orange, and green shag that she called spilled-taco style, or the inept air conditioner, but she would take care of those things when she had more time and money.

Patricia went to the small, windowless back room where she kept her supplies, photocopy machine, and filing cabinets—red files for active cases, blue for closed. She also kept a few concessions to body and soul: mini-refrigerator; microwave; blanket, overnight kit, and change of clothes, for those few occasions when she worked far enough into the morning hours to justify staying overnight; and a copy of the *Tao Te Ching*.

Patricia got out a fresh manila folder for the Andy Lawson

report, then on impulse pulled out the red file labeled *Kauffman, hatpins*. The file in front of it was labeled *Kauffman, missing agent*. She had decided to keep the cases separate, since by all appearances they were, although each file held a duplicate of her notes from the first interview with Elsa.

She thumbed past the notes in the *Kauffman, hatpins* file and skimmed the information she had found on Friedrich. He was, at least by every legal standard, the moral antithesis of his missing employee. Friedrich's pristine records reflected a steadiness of life unusual in the modern world; he had remained in the same business and same house for nearly thirty years. From a database specializing in public property records, Patricia had learned that Friedrich owned an impressive number of rental offices, apartments, and houses. Back in the late 1940s he had started making his fortune by developing Eagle Rise Estates, a plat of middle-class homes, with a partner, Russell Knepper.

While the official records on Friedrich were clean, a few articles about him in the *Cincinnati Enquirer*, which Patricia searched in a database of newspapers, hinted at a different Friedrich. He had created a few enemies when he auctioned off several farms at a low price, then bought them back from the person he'd sold them to, a person he had allegedly hired to buy the land as a front for him. Then he developed the land with high-priced homes, raising complaints that he'd stopped the auctions too early to allow for bids of real value so he'd make a fatter profit. The complaints had never been proven. One letter to the editor from a man named Leroy Hibberd had been particularly harsh against Friedrich, suggesting, without elaborating, that this was not the first time the Kauffman family had been in trouble.

Patricia put the file away, went back up front, tucked the Andy Lawson report in the manila folder, put the folder in her briefcase, and headed for the door. She was anxious to meet Friedrich, to find out what the man behind the computer data was really like.

* * *

Patricia had imagined Friedrich Kauffman would be a large man: balding, belly over belt, red-faced, huffing with good-old-boy guffaws. He was none of those things.

Friedrich offered no expression; it appeared that he could not, for his colorless skin was taut over an angular and prominently boned skull, as if his skin had just stretched to fit. The only lines in his face, around his mouth and under his eyes, looked as if they had been carved there, rather than worn in with years of reaction. His shock of white hair was combed back from his high forehead. He held his head high, yet his shoulders bowed forward, as if time and gravity long had held a special need to push him toward the earth, while he had spent his life resisting them.

Friedrich's translucent blue eyes more than compensated for his frozen demeanor. Those eyes regarded Patricia with bemusement and contempt, as if she had been sent to him for appraisal and was already found lacking.

Friedrich, a tall, thin man, stood up and awkwardly used his left hand to shake Patricia's hand. Then Patricia saw that his right arm was gone from the elbow down.

"Miss Delaney, so nice to meet you," Friedrich said, sitting back down.

Patricia took a chair across from his desk, opened her briefcase, and pulled out her report on Andy Lawson. "Patricia, please," she said.

Friedrich pressed his lips together in an unsmiling line. "Very well," he said, not pleased with the suggestion of informality. He studied her, and Patricia found she had to extract her eyes from his.

She looked down at his desk. The few items on it—a legal form of some sort, a file folder, a leatherbound appointment book, a calculator—were set at perfect right angles. The office was Spartan, the monotony of its white walls broken only by a few generic nature paintings.

Patricia considered how to proceed—let him ask the questions, or start in on a summary for him? She rubbed the white diagonal scar on her chin.

Friedrich cleared his throat, and Patricia looked up, realizing belatedly, with a sinking in her chest, that she had responded to the sound as to a command.

"You appear competent enough. My daughter Elsa described you that way, and she's usually a good judge of character. She recommended Andy to me."

Patricia's throat tightened while her hands clenched, crunching the folder. How the hell was she supposed to deliver a report on Andy Lawson after that? It would either make Elsa look incompetent as a judge of character, put herself in the same light as Andy, or both.

"I take it you didn't hire a private investigator to check into Andy's background, or any of your other agents?" Patricia said finally.

"No, of course not—"

"It would have been a good idea. The best judges of character have been fooled by many a con. One of the things these people rely on is their ability to appear totally charming and trustworthy."

"Are you saying you've learned Andy Lawson is a con?" Friedrich's voice was bemused. Was he amused by the suggestion that Andy was a con, or by how she had handled his opening insinuation about her competence?

"Not exactly. But I've done an extensive check into his background, and it's less than clean." Patricia put the manila folder on Friedrich's desk. "The details are in there, if you care to review them. I've found a few contacts—family and friends—and am gathering more. He'll turn up with family members or friends, or open an account with the money he took. Presuming he did take it. I recommend a background check on all your other employees. We're assuming that Andy's and the money's disappearance aren't coincidence. Most likely they aren't, but I always like to be sure."

Friedrich put his fingertips on the edge of the manila folder, pulled it toward him, then pushed it away.

"No. Andy took the money. Checking my other people will not be necessary. I only want him found so he can tell me why he took it."

"He was the only one who had access to the safe, then. Besides yourself and Elsa, of course."

"What do you mean?"

"To take the money he had to have access to the safe, or be working with someone who did."

"Everyone here has access to the safe. I trust all my employees. We are like family here." Friedrich spoke evenly, his eyes steadily pinned on Patricia.

She forced her eyes not to waver from his. "I can see that." Except this so-called family member apparently had taken one fat cookie from the family cookie jar. "You're sure it was Andy?"

"He's missing. No one would steal and remain behind, would they, Miss Delaney?"

"I've learned that people do all kinds of things."

"I do not want my other people or business pried into. Find Andy. He'll have the money."

Patricia took a deep breath, exhaling slowly to calm herself. So that was how Friedrich's world operated. He knew the answers. Others existed to prove him right.

"Let me ask you this, then, Mr. Kauffman. Why did you have one hundred thousand dollars cash in your safe? That's an incredible amount—"

"It's for personal business. I'd asked Elsa to take it from our basic bank account and leave it for me. I'd intended to take care of it as soon as she had the cash. Unfortunately I've been busy lately and my daughter neglected to find me as soon as possible. Otherwise this would not have happened."

Patricia was sure Elsa had been made to feel the full extent of her father's cold wrath, to squirm under his unyielding gaze as she demonstrated a sufficient measure of remorse for the grossness of her error. Patricia was equally sure that she would not learn from Friedrich the nature of his personal business.

"So over a period of what—one or two days perhaps— anyone could have seen the money and taken it from the safe."

Friedrich's pale eyebrows pulled together in a frown. "Find

Andy. If Andy took it, I'm sure there is a very good explanation and he will give it to me. If he did not, we'll proceed from there later.''

Friedrich picked up a sheet of paper and began reading it over. Then he put it down and began entering numbers on the calculator, glancing back at the paper occasionally. Patricia was, she realized, dismissed, but she did not get up. She looked evenly at Friedrich.

"Do you have any enemies, Mr. Kauffman?"

Friedrich finished his calculation, then looked up at her slowly. "Enemies? Why do you ask that?"

She thought of the hatpins and their messages in her desk. Elsa had thought her father would be amused by her concern over them. Patricia wondered if instead he'd be incensed that anyone would choose to taunt him so obliquely. Or would he be frightened, masking that fright with the indifferent amusement Elsa had envisioned?

"It helps in any investigation to know who the client's enemies are," she said.

Friedrich stared at her for a long moment, his look not really seeing or observing her, but taking her in, bit by bit. The sensation of being mentally consumed sent a chill dancing over her skin.

"You may have noticed that my right arm is missing from the elbow down," Friedrich said.

"Yes."

"I lost it when I was two, an accident in the street in Germany. I crippled my right leg, too. It was not long before my mother and I came here." Friedrich settled back in his chair, obviously relishing the story he was about to tell.

"My father had a jewelry and clock shop. Not long after I was crippled, some thugs tried to rob his shop. I don't remember this, mind you. My mother always liked to tell me the story. She said he tried to protect the shop because he had told her the shop would be my future—with just one arm and a crippled leg, I would be limited."

"My father, who had fought without injury in the first great war, resisted the robbers," Friedrich continued. "He was killed. The robbers fled without taking much. Not long after, my mother and I moved here to Cincinnati to live with her older brother, who had been here for years. So you see, unlike my father, I cannot fight.''

Friedrich leaned across his desk, looked directly into Patricia's eyes, and repeated, ''I cannot fight. And so, my dear, I have been certain to develop no enemies.''

He relaxed again into his chair, permitting himself at last the smile he had only been hinting at throughout their interview. The slow, deliberate smile made his face seem even more rigid, as if every facial muscle were pulled and frozen to sustain it. It was a smile that proclaimed the rarity of both its appearance and of its intent to inspire trust. It was a smile that then mocked you for even considering trusting it. It was a smile that took pleasure in your shock at that fact. Friedrich held the smile for a few seconds, then dropped it.

He picked up the phone, punched a number.

''Come to my office,'' he commanded, then hung up. He looked away from Patricia and back at his papers, which he started shuffling through. ''Elsa can help you with any other questions you have.''

Patricia exhaled slowly. She hadn't realized until then that she had been holding her breath, or that her brow was covered with cold sweat. She took the manila file on Andy Lawson from Friedrich's desk, gathered her briefcase and purse, stood, and turned to go. With a start she saw Elsa in the doorway of her father's office. Patricia hadn't even heard the door open. But Elsa waited for her, silent as a shadow.

Chapter 4

Elsa punched the numbers into the calculator, paused before totaling, sighed in frustration, unsure whether or not she had actually entered all the numbers correctly, pressed clear for the third time, and started over. She was waiting for Patricia to come to her office, and that made her nervous.

When Patricia left Friedrich's office, Elsa had noted the expression she tried to cover with a smile—stunned dismay—and had immediately felt a surge of empathy. She had wanted to say something, anything, but could only offer Patricia a weak smile and escort her down to the office area to Andy's desk. Patricia had said she would look through Andy's desk, then come back up to her office and talk with her.

That had been forty-five minutes ago, and Elsa had spent the time alternately on work and on the inexplicably anxious hope that Patricia could tell her who had been sending the hatpins. She didn't want the mystery to go on much longer; it weighed on her, making her tense and restless at night as she tried to sleep.

Elsa put aside the calculator and papers and glanced around her office, her eyes unable to settle on anything personal or soothing, because there was nothing of the kind in the room. Whereas Friedrich's office was neat because it was almost empty, Elsa's was neat because she had imposed order upon it. The numerous papers on the desk and on the credenza behind it were carefully stacked, corners evenly aligned. Everything on the desk—stapler, tape holder, pencil holder, phone—was lined up like a group of good little soldiers waiting to be called into duty, waiting to help control and organize all the paperwork that came through Elsa's office. The only picture was a generic nature scene, a copy of the boat-and-ocean picture hanging in her father's office, and its only purpose was to conceal the wall safe.

But there was nothing personal in the office. Elsa had worked for her father's business for twenty-three years and had never seen the need for anything personal—houseplant, photos, cute or funny paperweights, or even a mug. She had a cup of tea in the morning and another in the afternoon, which she drank in ten minutes or less from a white Styrofoam cup in the kitchen downstairs. Her personality was not needed at the office, just her skills.

Still, she sometimes smiled secretly at the knowledge of the little flower patch she tended next to the back patio. The flower bed had already been there, overgrown with weeds when Friedrich took over the house in an older section of Blue Ash rezoned for business and converted it into an office ten years before, and she had felt an obligation to do something with it. It was really for the agents' enjoyment, she told herself and her father.

A knock came at the door. Elsa stood up, smoothed her skirt, and cleared her throat. "Come in," she said.

Patricia entered, shutting the door behind her, and took the chair in front of Elsa's desk.

"Did you—did you find everything you need?" Elsa asked.

"Yes. I looked through Andy's desk thoroughly—nothing there unexpected or unusual. Except this." Patricia handed Elsa a sheet. It was a photocopy of a page from Andy's memo pad, with just an out-of-town phone number.

"I wouldn't have thought anything of it," Patricia said, "except it's the same number Andy left by his phone at his apartment, right before he left, apparently to come in here one night. It was the last time his roommate has seen or heard from him. The roommate didn't know what the number was for. Do you?"

"Yes. It's for the Mermaid Mirage Motel in Orlando, Florida. Where Kurt Knepper is staying on vacation. I made the reservations for him myself. Kurt is our newest agent.''

"Knepper. Friedrich developed a large neighborhood of homes—Eagle Rise Estates—back in the late 1940s with a Russell Knepper.''

"Kurt's father. Russell and my father were cousins.''

"Do you think Andy could be in Florida? Maybe he and Kurt, working together, came up with the idea of taking the hundred grand.''

"No—oh no. Kurt is family. Andy was covering clients for Kurt, that's all. Probably called to ask him a question or two. Kurt has some—picky clients right now, the Aberdeens. Nothing suits them. And anyway Kurt and Andy aren't close, even though they share a desk. That's why Andy is—was—is covering for Kurt.''

"Because they share a desk?''

"Yes. Deskmates cover for one another. We don't want any client to feel he or she isn't getting the best possible service,'' Elsa said confidently. That was what all the brochures and fliers on the business said.

"Why don't they get along?'' Patricia asked.

"Andy is—flamboyant. Kurt is quieter.''

"Withdrawn?''

"No. Just reserved.''

"Maybe he took the money before he went down to Florida. Andy found out about it and went down to get a piece of the pie. So to speak.''

"No,'' Elsa said. "Like I said, Kurt is family. He lived with us for a while after his—parents died. It was—very tragic. He was like another brother, another son, for a while.''

"I see,'' Patricia said quietly, her bemused expression betraying her disbelief.

Elsa felt her throat tightening as it always did at any potential disagreement. Patricia's calm, relaxed smile didn't help. It was easy enough for her to question the ways of the Kauffman business and family. She hadn't been drilled all these years about the tight-knit Kauffman family, about how that closeness should—would—permeate the business. Conspiracies or rebellions were not possible in the business or family where Friedrich ruled.

"Speaking of family, I met your sister downstairs."

Elsa licked her dry lips and tucked a stray strand of hair behind her ears. "Brenda. Yes."

Elsa knew what Patricia must be thinking—quite a shocking contrast, the Kauffman sisters. To Elsa, Brenda was the blond, glamorous one, who wore silky blouses and tight skirts, jewelry and high-heeled shoes, makeup and perfume.

"She was talking with a man, a Tom Nielson, in the kitchen when I went to photocopy the page from Andy's memo pad."

"Tom. Yes. Tom Nielson is Father's development partner." Elsa cleared her throat and continued more assuredly. "He and my father are working together on a new development in the east suburban area of Cinci—near Eagle Rise, my father's first development. This one will be called Brookshire Estates. Tom's developed other planned communities—Nottingham Woods, for one. They're two- to three-hundred-thousand-dollar custom-built homes, for people of discriminating taste." That was from the flier and sales brochure currently at the printer. Elsa offered a tentative smile.

"I'm not in the market, Elsa," Patricia said. "I just want to know a little about Tom's relationship with your father."

"Oh. Well, Tom's—Tom's the expert in the partnership. He's done developments of this sort, this size, the contracting, planning, marketing. My father is the financial backing. This will be his first development with a partner since Eagle Rise."

"Why?" Patricia asked.

"Why?" Elsa fingered her throat nervously.

"Yes. Why no partners after Eagle Rise, until now?"

"I—I'm not sure I—"

"Elsa, if you want me to help you, you're going to have to trust me."

Elsa cleared her throat. She wasn't sure how much to tell Patricia; she was sure, however, that her father would be angry if he knew she was revealing this much. But she needed to trust someone.

"Eagle Rise ended—tragically. Russell Knepper was hot-headed, from what I've heard. I don't remember any of this; I was too young. My grandmother told me later. He—he got angry one night, in a jealous rage, and killed his wife. Later he killed himself in jail. The media attention was awful. After that Father preferred to work alone."

"Until now, when he's decided to take Tom as a partner."

"Yes. Brenda recommended him, I believe."

"And there are no conflicts between them, I suppose."

"No . . ."

"Just wondered. I overheard Tom telling Brenda that he'd had it up to here with your father's interference. Brenda, unfortunately, shut him up when she saw me, and Tom stormed out. That's when Brenda introduced herself to me." Patricia leaned across the desk toward Elsa. "I'm just trying to determine who might possibly be angry enough to send your father threatening notes on hatpins. According to you and your father, he has no enemies, so this is quite a mystery to me."

"You didn't mention the ha-hatpins to Brenda, did you?" Patricia leaned back in her chair and sighed. "No."

"Good. I don't—don't think it would be Tom. He's just nervous now with all that's going on. Have you found out anything about them? About the hatpins, I mean?"

Patricia shook her head. "I'm going to the shop—Rosie's Attic—tomorrow to talk to the owner. Other than that I have been too busy trying to find Andy Lawson and the hundred thousand dollars for you. Which leads me to another question. Do you know why your father had a hundred thousand dollars cash in the safe?"

Elsa swallowed hard, trying to get past the lump in her throat. "No." She swallowed again, licking her lips. "No, I don't. Sometimes, once or twice a year or so, he asks me to pull that amount, maybe more, for him."

"And what does he tell you to track the money under in your books?"

"Overhead."

Patricia pressed her lips together and studied Elsa's expression. She doesn't believe me, thought Elsa. She thinks I know something. . . . The phone rang. Elsa picked it up immediately, relieved to have something to break up the conversation.

Her relief quickly turned to tension, however. It was her father. "Yes. Yes, Father," she said. Elsa kept mumbling "yes," hoping that would mask her father's voice. Patricia could surely hear him, yelling on the other end. Elsa hated this, mumbling "yes," nodding her head like she was dodging blows. She chanced a glance at Patricia and was relieved to see that she found the ship-and-ocean picture interesting enough to study.

Finally her father let her go. Elsa hung up and coughed nervously. Patricia looked back at her, smiling carefully, and the carefulness of that smile, which Elsa suspected hid pity, made her more embarrassed. She cleared her throat and began fingering the yellow scarf tied in a lopsided bow at her neck. "Father. He was—disappointed in how long I've taken in organizing the details for this auction tomorrow. I—I have taken longer than usual."

Patricia nodded, as if she understood. "I'll let you know how the meeting with the antique-shop owner goes." She put the photocopy of Andy's memo pad in her briefcase and stood up. "Give me a call if you need anything." She gathered her things and headed for the door.

"Oh, Patricia?" Elsa said.

"Yes."

"Have you ever been to an auction?"

"No."

"You might enjoy seeing one—this one tomorrow. It's out in the country—a farmer's house—here's a flier."

Patricia took the flier, glanced at it, and tucked it in a side pocket of her briefcase.

"Thanks, but I don't think I can make it." She smiled gently. "I'm going to the antique shop tomorrow, and then to pick up an out-of-town guest at the bus station. My niece."

"Oh. How nice. Well—"

"I'll be in touch, Elsa," Patricia said, and left, closing the door after her.

For a few moments Elsa sat silently, unmoving. Then she went back to the calculator, losing herself in the safe neutrality of her work.

Elsa stood in the doorway to the family room, watching her father. It was after eight, and she had just finished cleaning up the dinner dishes. She had wanted to ask him a question about the upcoming auction, but Friedrich was asleep in his recliner, snoring lightly, his face slack and relaxed like it never was when he was awake. The book he was reading, another volume on World War I, was open, facedown on his chest.

As Elsa watched him the hateful thought came welling up in her mind before she could prevent it, as it had many times before. It would be so simple to take the needlepointed rose cushion on the couch and press it over his face, stifling at last and forever his snoring, his breath, him.

She pushed the thought down with more shame than horror, swallowing it back like bitter bile, ashamed that she hadn't been able to catch the thought in time to suppress it. She comforted herself, as she always did, with the belief that they didn't really matter, these forbidden thoughts that sometimes came to her like strange desires, dancing flames that drew her to them. The thoughts were hers alone, no one but she knew them, and once her life was over and done with, they would be snuffed out as if they had never been.

She went back to the small kitchen, which smelled of the fried sausage and onions and stewed tomatoes she had made for their supper. The smell was stiflingly heavy for a summer's evening, and Elsa opened the window. Then she knelt down, wiped up a spot of stewed tomatoes from the kitchen floor, white tile with green and silver specks. She'd always wanted to redo the homely floor, but her mother had never wanted to alter anything about the house, and now that she was dead it would seem irreverent to go ahead with the change.

Elsa filled a glass with iced tea and went back out to the family room, moving quietly so as not to disturb her father. She sat at the end of the brown couch, putting the needle-pointed cushion—one of the last her grandmother had done—to the small of her back. She picked up the historical romance from the end table and tried to read. Friedrich's snoring was disturbing, but it didn't occur to her to go upstairs to her room for some peace and quiet.

They always sat together in the family room, every night after dinner. She read or listened to her father talk on some point of the auctioneering or real-estate business; Friedrich read or talked or napped or watched television. It was the pattern they had followed when her mother was alive. Elsa had stayed in the room with them, available to fetch a drink or pillow or medicine or snack for them, since her mother had been sickly and unable to care for herself or Friedrich.

Changing the pattern after her mother's death five years before had not occurred to either Elsa or Friedrich. He wanted the same comforts he had gotten used to, and Elsa had never developed any interests to pursue in the evenings except reading her romance novels. Her grandmother Gertrude had always disapproved of them, saying they weren't realistic, nothing like the real romance she had had with her husband until he was killed.

Elsa tried to concentrate, but she couldn't seem to relax enough to be swept away as the cover promised. She kept thinking of Patricia. Patricia, she thought, wouldn't understand any of this. Patricia was the sort of woman Elsa wanted to be long ago when she went to Alliston College, and knew she would never be—independent. Tough. Smart. Pretty. Capable of maintaining, without guilt or defensiveness, an allegiance to herself, to her own needs and desires and pleasures.

And Patricia would laugh at her for thinking that, tell her she was idealizing her too much, and wonder why Elsa couldn't just get up and leave the house if that was what she wanted.

Because we're all so close, we're such a tight-knit family, thought Elsa. It was a message their parents had drilled into her and her siblings, smiling as they said it. Yet there was always something—a glance, a lifted eyebrow, a sigh, that showed that what their children did and said wasn't quite enough and was never going to be. The Kauffman children— simply because they were children, and children always hope to please—nevertheless clung to the belief that something they said or did might redeem them, if they tried hard enough.

Henry, the oldest and the only son, had wounded his father irreparably by becoming a lawyer and disassociating himself from the family business except for occasional legal counsel. Sometimes someone, like Andy, would come along and fill in as a surrogate son for Friedrich, which made Friedrich calmer and easier to get along with for a time. But such a person was always marked to somehow fall into disfavor and be dismissed from the family fold. Andy was unique only in that he probably had really done something wrong.

Brenda, the middle child, was her father's favorite. She had devoted herself completely to the business—one reason her marriage had failed, since her husband and kids had wanted her around some of the time. When they saw that they came in a distant second, they left. Brenda's response had been to get her auctioneer's license, to serve as a backup to Friedrich, something he'd been asking her to do for years.

And Elsa . . . well, she had known, had somehow always known, that apart from her family she would dissolve, absorbed unnoticed into the stream of humanity. At least with them she had always been needed for something. Yet now her father seemed to disdain her, to be so disappointed in her. But it hadn't always been that way. The hatpins—those strange figures with the vaguely threatening notes—the hatpins reminded her.

She didn't remember them specifically at all from her childhood, and yet the hatpins seemed to lull her into thinking about the distant past. Elsa thought of a long-ago time—

she must have been only seven or younger—when she was
her father's favorite. She would dress up in her grandmother's
old clothes from the trunk in the attic and model for him. He
would laugh then, scoop her up with his one arm, and call
her—what was it he called her? His "little angel." That was
it. Her mother and older siblings glared at her jealously, but
it didn't matter to her then.

Then came the night when everything inexplicably
changed. She had been sleeping poorly and woke up in the
middle of the night to hear a noise downstairs, and she knew
with the instinct of a child that it was her father. In her fuzzy
half-awake state, she realized he had stormed out of the house
earlier, angry, and had not come up to kiss her and her siblings good night like he always did, and his absence had left
her sleep riddled with nightmares. She saw, draped over the
back of a rocker, the dark shapes of the dress-up clothes she
had modeled earlier in the day, making her father laugh and
call her "little angel." So she slipped out of bed, careful not
to disturb Brenda sleeping next to her, and put on the dress
over her cotton nightgown, and the big hat.

She got down to the kitchen and saw him there, a big man
to a child's eyes, filling the kitchen, standing with his feet
wide apart on the green-and-silver-specked linoleum, just the
buzzing light over the kitchen sink on, scrubbing his hands.
He was mumbling to himself, and she realized he was still
angry.

She said "Papa," that was all, and smiled, waiting for
him to turn to her and laugh and not be angry anymore. But
when he turned and looked at her, fixing her to the spot on
the kitchen floor as immovably as if she were one of the silver
or green specks, she saw him as she never had before, but
would for the rest of her life. He was unsmiling, his mouth
set and hard, his eyes cold and angry. The front of his shirt
was messy—with what she wasn't sure—but she knew that
because of it he wouldn't be picking her up now and calling
her "little angel," he wouldn't be picking her up ever again,
and she shrank from him, ready to turn and run back up the
stairs.

He smacked her across the face and grabbed her arm when she started shaking. Her mouth gaped silently, and she knew she must not cry out. Then he spoke to her—in her panic she could not understand him, but she instinctively knew later never to mention that night to him or anyone else—and when he finally released her, she turned and ran, sliding back into bed without taking off the dress. The hat had fallen off as she ran up the stairs, but it was on the dresser the next morning.

After that night things somehow permanently changed— at least so it seemed to Elsa. Surely it was only in a child's mind that things could change that suddenly; surely it had only been gradually, bit by bit, that her father found her less amusing, increasingly awkward and stupid, while her mother and sister and brother, sensing her fallen status, pounced on the chance to join in with relish, revenge for all the times he had praised her and not them. She was a fallen angel, the stupid, slow, fearing, gawky one, somewhat embarrassing, a child to send off on tasks and errands and otherwise ignore.

Elsa started, realizing she had been drifting half in sleep and half in memory. She tried to go back to her book, but thinking of the past made her think of her grandmother, and how she always talked about her husband. Friedrich's father had been tall and handsome and perfect, so brave when he fought in World War I.

When her grandmother died, her father put nearly everything—her house, and all its contents—on the auction block. He had been puritanical in his zeal to get rid of his mother's belongings. There were only a few things in Friedrich's house that had been her grandmother's—the needlepoint rose pillow, a vase, and the box up in the attic that Friedrich didn't know about.

It contained things that would never have sold at auction anyway, except perhaps some of the postcards for collectors of such—her grandfather's letters from the front, diaries, photo albums, other letters, scrapbooks. Friedrich didn't know she had kept the box. She had wanted to look through it carefully for a long time, but had never gotten up the nerve.

Just sneaking it up to the attic a year ago had seemed treacherous enough.

And then Elsa thought of Patricia. Patricia would tell her to go look through the box if she wanted to, for heaven's sake.

Friedrich would be sleeping for a long time, and if he woke and called for her, she would be able to hear him and could tell him she had been doing some cleaning upstairs.

Elsa put her book aside, got up, and headed to the attic. The hatpins had made her attracted to the past in a curious way. And so it was, Elsa decided, time to take a look through the box.

Chapter 5

The antique shop was in a row of buildings, some former homes, that Patricia thought of as "early gingerbread"—plenty of ornate gables, cornices, porches, and perky bright paint meant to charm city visitors on weekends. The two-story yellow house that was now home to Rosie's Attic was not quite in disrepair, but in need of a good surface cleanup—a fresh coat of paint, minor repairs to sagging steps and shutters, maybe a few pots of plants.

Patricia maneuvered her black Chevy S-10 pickup between two cars along the curb across the street from Rosie's Attic. She rolled down the truck's window to let in some air, then snapped open her briefcase on the passenger's seat. She pulled out the file marked *Kauffman, hatpins*.

Patricia flipped open the file, ran her index finger along the margin of the notes she had written up on her computer. Rosie Sanderson, owner of Rosie's Attic, antique shop in Lebanon, Ohio, had bought the hatpins originally at Elsa's grandmother's funeral almost a year before. From a quick search of Rosie's name and business, Patricia was able to learn that Rosie had died about eight months ago, leaving Aaron, her husband, as sole owner of the business. Patricia looked back out at the shop. Aaron apparently didn't have the love or energy for the shop that Rosie probably had. A grimy sign was stuck on the porch column: OPEN, 1:00. Patricia checked her watch. It was 1:30 now, but the place didn't look open. She closed up her briefcase and took it with her out of the truck and across the street.

Patricia glanced in a window that was opaque with gummy

41

dirt and noted the vague shapes in the display window: a rocker, in which was propped an old-fashioned stuffed bunny in a calico dress; an antique sewing machine; a floor lamp with tassels hanging from the shade. Feeling like she really was about to enter someone's personal attic, she turned the knob and pushed open the door.

It swung open with a protesting squeal. Patricia stepped in and let the door slam shut behind her. It took a few seconds to adjust to the dimness after the bright midday sun and to the smell of mustiness. Patricia worked her way back through the long narrow store, past old typewriters and furniture, a rack of old clothes from the thirties and forties, desks piled with mildewing books and magazines, and piles of old jewelry, some paste, some high quality. She paused at a dresser on top of which were stacked old hats, but no hatpins. At the back of the store was an opening overhung with an old red velvet curtain.

"Hello?" Patricia called out. She heard a rustling from behind the curtain, then silence, then more rustling as a small, hunchbacked man came out from behind the curtain, which sent up a puff of dust as it fell back in place.

The old man, with just a mussed tuft of white hair on top of his head, looked around frowning.

"Over here," Patricia said.

He turned at the sound of her voice and peered up at her. He pushed his glasses up on his face. They immediately slid down again.

"Why, hello! Is there something I can help you with?" His voice was strong and clear, registering surprise at seeing someone in his shop.

"Yes, I think so. I hope so anyway. My name is Patricia Delaney—"

"Nice to meet you, dear," the old man said, smiling at her now. He held out his hand. She accepted his handshake, which was much stronger than she had expected.

"Thank you. I take it you're Aaron Sanderson?"

"Why, yes." He seemed surprised that anyone would know who he was.

"Good. I need to talk with you. I'm a private investigator, and my client wanted me to help her find out about some hatpins that were purchased here."

Aaron blinked at Patricia. "Your client needs a jewelry appraiser if she wants to know what they're really worth. I have a little jewelry around, but I'm no expert. That was Rosie's interest. Now, furniture, if you want to know about that—like this nice dresser—" He patted the top of a dresser and looked at her anxiously, inviting her to ask questions.

Patricia smiled. "Not today. I just need some help with these hatpins. Maybe if you took a look at them. . . ." Patricia put her briefcase on a clear edge of the dresser, opened it, and got out a small cardboard box. She closed the briefcase, then opened the box and got out the hatpins and put them down on the dresser. She had left the messages that came with them safely back in her office. Aaron adjusted his glasses, which promptly slid down again, and squinted down at the hatpins.

"According to my client's records, your wife bought these about a year ago. At an auction put on by Kauffman Real Estate and Auctioneers, in Cincinnati," Patricia said.

The old man didn't say anything. He stared down at the hatpins with the same fascination and almost reluctant awe that Elsa had shown in Patricia's office.

"There were twelve hatpins total, all from the Victorian era." Patricia paused, starting to lose hope that she was going to get any information from Aaron. "Is there anything at all you can tell me about them?" she asked.

Aaron looked up at her, his pale blue eyes suddenly sharp and questioning. He studied her warily, carefully pushing his glasses up on the bridge of his nose, apparently unaware of them almost immediately sliding down again to the tip of his nose.

"What did you say you are, a lawyer?"

"Private investigator."

"Who did you say your client was?"

Patricia grinned. The old man was sharper than he let on.

"I didn't. Do you know if your wife did purchase these at the auction for Gertrude Kauffman about a year ago?"

Aaron nodded. "Yes. We both went. Rosie wanted to go— she always read the auction pages. One of Rosie's favorite things to do, you know." Aaron glanced beyond Patricia's shoulder and chuckled. "Always told her she just had this shop because she couldn't stop buying old stuff and there wasn't enough room in our house for everything."

Patricia could tell it was going to be difficult to keep Aaron nudged gently on track. "That's interesting, Mr. Sanderson. So you purchased these hatpins for the shop. . . ."

Aaron focused on Patricia again. "That's right. Well, Rosie did. I went with her to the auction, though. She didn't like to drive at the end. A dozen, all told. A dozen hatpins. None of them the same, except there was a twin to this one." He picked up the death-smiling angel, gave it a twirl, then immediately put it down, frowning at it like it disturbed him for some unnamable reason.

"And someone bought them from you."

"Yes, but I'm afraid I never saw him. Rosie was still alive then and running the shop. She just passed away eight months ago. God rest her soul."

"I'm sorry to hear that, Mr. Sanderson," Patricia said, even though she already knew that to be the case. She did not like to always reveal just how much she learned about people from her computer searches. It made some people uncomfortable, some angry, and it was always interesting to see how much people were willing to reveal about themselves on their own. You could learn something, at least, about a person's character that way.

"Thank you, dear. Rosie told me all about the customer who bought the hatpins after the advertising flier she sent him came back with no such address on it. Young man, she said, clean-cut and handsome. Like a regular gentleman, she said." Aaron paused to chuckle. "That was one of her phrases. Regular gentleman. He came in just the day after the auction, looked around, then asked her about hatpins. She was taken aback, she said. She'd never had hatpins before, and bought them on a lark because she thought they were pretty. But Rosie always kept a straight face. Could have been a regular poker player, if it hadn't been against her religion. But she never minded me playing on a Thursday night. . . ." Aaron stared off in space, back at a different time when his Rosie was still alive.

"So she got out the hatpins to show the man," Patricia urged gently.

"Yes. From the back area here." Aaron waved in the direction of the curtain he had come out from under. "It's where we keep stuff not ready for the shop yet. She hadn't even gotten out the hatpins yet. She was going to make a display of them on a hat. But she never got a chance. She just unwrapped them, showed them to the man, and he bought them all on the spot. Just like that. Just barely looked them over and didn't even try to haggle."

"Did she by chance get a name from him—a reason why he wanted the hatpins?"

"No reasons. But she got a name. She got him to sign the guest register. Rosie was always big on that—get a name and address and send a flier every few months to the ones who live nearby to get them to come in. She told me he was real friendly about the whole thing seemed so tickled to have these hatpins. Such a nice man, she said. He said he'd be happy to get her fliers. He'd come back often, he said."

Aaron shook his head. "That was the thing that got Rosie. A month later the flier came back—no such address. She tried again, tried to find the correct address. That was Rosie, you see. It bothered her—he'd seemed eager to get the fliers. And she couldn't believe he'd given her a false address just to be nice, but didn't really want the fliers."

"It sounds like it bothered her a great deal," Patricia said.

Aaron nodded. "It worried her, you know, and the worry worked on her. A few months later she got the cancer. That's why it sticks in my mind. She still kept talking about the man and the hatpins. Maybe it was something she used to distract herself from the cancer. I don't know. It's like those hatpins were a curse.'' Aaron stared at them, like he wanted to spit on them.

"I'm sorry, Mr. Sanderson," Patricia said. "Do you still have the register the man signed?"

Aaron looked back up at her. "Yes, oh yes. Me and Rosie—never threw anything out. Lived through the Depression, you know. And it was important to Rosie. Still working on filling it out, you know?"

Patricia scooped up the hatpins in the box, and followed Aaron as he started up to the front of the shop. He went behind a cluttered counter and pushed a tattered green logbook at her. He opened it up and started thumbing through the pages. He stopped near the end.

"There were only a few names after his. I'll recognize it when I see it. Rosie talked about him enough." He moved back one page, then pointed a quivering finger at a name.

Jack Grierson, 312 Forest Avenue, Dayton, Ohio. *Nice shop,* he'd written in the column for comments. The handwriting was precise and nondescript, in block letters, suggesting a person who had studied drafting. Patricia doubted the style was naturally Jack's—or whoever had written this.

Patricia got her notebook out of her briefcase, then wrote down the name and address, double-checked it, then put it back in her briefcase. She looked up at Aaron, ready to say thank you and good-bye.

Aaron was looking at her eagerly. "Would you mind signing the book? I don't have to send you a flier if you don't want one, but I try to keep this tradition going. For Rosie."

Patricia smiled. "I'd be glad to. And I've love a flier." She plucked a pen out of her purse and signed the guest register. Then she got out a business card and gave it to Aaron.

"I put my home address in the book. That's my office address and number. If you remember anything else about this man, please give me a call."

Aaron looked at the card, then up at Patricia. He smiled. "I will."

"Thanks," Patricia said, and left the store.

On the way out of town Patricia stopped at a Dairy Queen and got a chocolate-dipped double vanilla cone. She had plenty of time before she had to get to the Greyhound bus station in Cincinnati to pick up Lucy.

She sat on a bench beneath a tree behind the DQ and watched a mother and her kids, under age six, at another bench. The kids' antics made Patricia smile and think about how Lucy had been at that age—mischievous, cheerful, fun. When she had last seen Lucy, five years before, she had been eleven years old, withdrawn, somber. Patricia wondered what she was like now. She'd find out soon enough.

As she licked her dipped double cone Patricia tried to think about what she would say or do with Lucy over the next few weeks, but her mind kept going back to Elsa and Friedrich and the hatpins.

It was difficult to imagine Elsa on her own, in Alliston at the college. What had she said she'd studied? Physics and chemistry, she had said, looking wistfully out the window as if she could see some floating mirage of the campus. Maybe, thought Patricia, this Jack Grierson had been a lover of Elsa's at college. Maybe she had given him her grandmother's hatpins for some reason, something had gone awry in the relationship, and now years later this Jack was sending the threatening hatpin notes.

Patricia dismissed the fanciful idea. She couldn't imagine Elsa with a lover. Even less could she imagine Elsa lying, saying she had never seen the hatpins before if she had. Patricia thought about how Elsa had acted as she discussed the hatpins. There were the nervous hands, playing with one another, the cloth of the faded, outdated dress, the thin, sharp voice that hesitantly repeated whatever it had just muttered in the conviction that surely no one was seriously listening.

Patricia frowned at herself as she finished off the cone. Stick to the real issue, she told herself, the missing agent and the money. She'd track the hatpins as far as she could because Elsa was paying her to, but most likely they were some kind of hoax, a prank perhaps from a disgruntled former employee.

Patricia got back in her truck, headed back to Cincinnati, and after she got on the highway, flipped on a classic rock station. She let the music wash over her mind and temporarily pushed away thoughts of Elsa or hatpins. Just down the road she had a niece to deal with.

Chapter 6

To fit in both the trip to Rosie's Attic and the Greyhound bus station that Saturday morning, Patricia had skipped her usual workout—a half mile at the pool at the Alliston College gym every morning, weight lifting every other morning. She rarely skipped her workouts, and now, sitting on a hard chair in the bus station, she felt restless and irritated because she had. The fact that she had arrived at the bus station a half hour before she had to, to pick up Lucy, also irritated her. She hated to admit it to herself, but the truth was she was nervous about this visit with her niece.

Patricia glanced around the bus station, which was mostly empty. A fresh-faced young girl, nose poked in a book in a manner that said "Please ignore me," sat by herself at the end of the row. A couple, also young but dressed in punk outfits meant to alarm, sat together on the floor in a corner. The boy strummed a guitar tunelessly.

Patricia closed her eyes and imagined herself lifting weights. She liked the swimming but really enjoyed lifting weights. It was like a physical form of meditation, focusing solely on the repetitions of a particular movement. And it was amazing how much easier it was to sit for twelve hours, waiting to see if a guy was going to come out of his workplace with something that wasn't his, if you were in good shape.

The noise of a bus arriving and passengers unloading broke through her concentration. Patricia opened her eyes and watched the crowd coming through the door—a mix of old and young, neat and sloppy, smiling and grumpy, but all of them bleary-eyed with the fatigue that comes from a long, slow journey.

Finally the only unclaimed people were an older man in a rumpled suit, looking around anxiously, and a young woman, looking bored. Patricia smiled to herself. Lucy.

Patricia studied her in the moments before she caught her eye, growing more amused as she looked. She remembered a petitely built child, fair-skinned, in neat dresses or pant suits, with light brown hair pulled back into barrettes or ponytails. Now here was the young woman, still petite and fair-skinned, but her hair dyed into a shock of pure midnight black, the complete blackness of witches' wigs sold at the five-and-dime around Halloween. Her hair was teased up in random directions at the back and falling into her eyes in front. Slashes of purple defined the hollows of her cheeks. Lucy wore all black—a T-shirt, a long cotton skirt, flat black sandals—and a heavy gold cross pendant and heavy gold cross earrings. The nun from hell, thought Patricia, smiling in amusement.

Their eyes met. Lucy didn't bother to return Patricia's smile, but stood holding her khaki duffel bag, looking a little anxious while trying to look bored. The nun from hell goes reluctantly to camp, thought Patricia. She walked over to her niece.

"Hi. I'm Patricia."

"Yeah. I remember you, Aunt Patricia."

"Just Patricia. Don't call me 'Aunt' anything, and I won't call you Lucinda." Lucy had hated being called by her full name as a child.

A smile teased around Lucy's lips, then quickly hid behind her noncommittal expression. "Sometimes I go by Lucky. What do you think of the nickname Lucky?"

"Great," said Patricia. "Is there anything else, or is your duffel bag it?"

"I'm glad you like the nickname. I made it up for myself on the bus because I'm sooo Lucky to be spending three weeks with you." Lucy finally smiled, but her grin was a sarcastic, taunting one.

It was going to be a long three weeks, thought Patricia, but she kept smiling and said, "Lucky is a great name. I used it when I was a strip dancer at an adult joint. Everyone wanted to get lucky, so I got great tips. Now, is the duffel bag it or what? I'm not asking again."

Lucy's face registered a mixture of shock and awe, then reverted to the safety of indifference. "The duffel bag's it."

"Then let's go." Patricia turned and started to the parking lot without waiting to see if Lucy was following her. Once on the road, with Lucy huddled against the passenger's door, hugging her bag and staring out the window, she finally relaxed a little.

It was a Saturday, the traffic winding around downtown wasn't too bad, and before long Patricia was up on the highway, cutting across northern Kentucky, then across the Ohio River and back into Ohio toward Alliston. The day was young: she and Lucy could come to terms—her terms—about life together for the next three weeks; the Reds were in town for a baseball game the next afternoon, maybe they'd go to that; she rarely went downtown, but maybe she'd take Lucy on a walking tour around Fountain Square or Yeatman's Cove; tonight she could take Lucy to Dean's Tavern. Lucy probably wouldn't care for the country-and-western band playing tonight, but it was as good a place as any to start showing her around Alliston.

"Were you really a stripper?" Lucy asked quietly.

Patricia smiled to herself before she answered. It had been a long time since she had thought about that, and there weren't too many people who knew about it. Her only reminder of that much younger, much wilder phase of her life came when she chanced a glimpse of her back, naked, in the mirror. She had a little yellow, red, and blue parrot tattooed on the right cheek of her butt.

"Yes, I really was. And my stage name really was Lucky. A long time ago, while I was in college. Club called Poppy's Parrot across the river in Newport, Kentucky." Cincinnati had purged itself of exotic dance clubs and porn shops long ago. Thrill seekers had to cross the river or drive to another city.

"Did you like it?"

Patricia shrugged. "It was okay. I made pretty good money, which I needed at the time."

"Weren't your parents upset?"

"I didn't tell them. One of my brothers—Ryan—found out when he came to visit me. He was furious until I assured him I didn't strip off completely, just down to a bikini swimsuit bottom. He still wasn't thrilled. But he hated what I did next even more."

"What was that?"

Patricia chuckled to herself. Lucy was hooked on the story. "I got smart—I got a job that paid better money. I became a bouncer."

"No way! How did you manage that? I mean I can't imagine a dancer going straight from the stage—"

"I'm just an inch shy of six feet. And I was pretty strong. Plus my brothers and dad had all insisted I—all of the girls—learn self-defense. I had to flip the club's owner over my shoulder and make him land hard on his back before he gave me the job, but he did."

Lucy was quiet after that. Patricia ventured a glance over at her. They were off the highway now, and she was staring out the window, watching the green, dense Ohio countryside roll by, punctuated every now and then by farmhouses, churches with little graveyards, or cornfields. Wild hair and weird clothes aside, Lucy seemed like a typical young woman, perhaps a little more scared, more confused than some, but she'd work through the phase—more than once, no doubt. Look at me, thought Patricia. From strip dancer to detective. The journey had been a good one.

"Too bad Mom never uses the self-defense Gramps and the uncles taught her. Sure she was paying attention at lesson time?" Lucy asked quietly.

Patricia sighed. "Ah yes. Maureen. How is your mother?"

"Fine, I guess. Finally found Prince Charming, right?"

"How big of a jerk is he?"

Lucy laughed. "You get to the point, don't you?"

"Sometimes."

"He's okay, I guess. Better than some of the others. So did Mom tell you about me?"

"Nah. She let me be shocked."

"I don't mean about my wardrobe. I mean about where I was just before I came down here."

"Playing tambourine with a South American band."

"Cute. Nope. Guess again."

Patricia sighed. She was too tired to play guessing games with a teenager. "Get to the point, Lucy."

"Okay. In jail. I was in jail."

"Well, you're here, so it couldn't have been too bad." Brother, thought Patricia. Was she really going to have to put up with three weeks of this kid playing Little Miss Tough Stuff? "What did you do, bash in a mailbox or two? Ram a stop sign?"

Lucy gave a staccato laugh. "Doesn't Mommy dear wish. Nope. Me and some friends knocked over a convenience store. Didn't get far with the money, but shit, we had fun. Judge would have probably gone lighter on me, 'cept I'd been up for shoplifting three times already. Those are the times they caught me. Cost Mommy dear's boyfriend a whole bunch to get me out this time." Lucy laughed again. "So whad'ya think, Auntie Patricia? This old guy must really like Mom. Or maybe she's just gotten better in the sack."

The truck wove a little to the right, and Patricia straightened it, forcing herself to keep control of her driving, breathing, and expression. She pushed back the impulse to stop the truck and smack Lucy. So that was why Maureen wanted to off-load her daughter for a while. It wouldn't take long for a smart ass, thieving teenager to drive away Maureen's boyfriend, really mucking up her plans to hit the big time with the latest sugar daddy.

" 'Course, my counselor says I do it for the attention. Maybe yes, maybe no. Personally I just like taking stuff. You'd be surprised at how easy it is."

"Okay, Lucinda, pay attention to this. You rip off any

stores while you're here, and I won't bail your ass out of jail. I'll do my best to convince the judge it should rest there a good long time. Got that?''

"Wow. You're just Miss Sympathy. My counselor says I need—"

"I'm not your counselor. And I don't have sympathy for people who like to feel sorry for themselves. You want attention from me, just say hello in the morning, good-bye when you leave for somewhere, thank you when I pass the butter at the dinner table.''

"Oh, yes, ma'am.''

"And cut the sarcasm—and the comments about your mother. Or you'll be on the next bus back to Detroit. You want to talk, fine, but I'm not playing pity-party games with you about how rough you've had it,'' Patricia said, although she was sure Lucy's life with Maureen hadn't been easy. "Understand?''

"Yeah. I understand,'' Lucy said, in a tone that meant, Of course I understand. You're a jerk, just like all the adults I know.

Lucy stared out the window again, hugging her duffel bag. Patricia felt a surge of sympathy, a wish to reach over and squeeze her arm and tell her things would be okay. But she had told Maureen that, long ago, and things hadn't worked out that way. For the first time in years she felt out of control of a situation. It was a strange feeling.

Patricia concentrated on the country scenery rolling by, houses, cornfields, churches, trees. It was silent until she heard a ding. She looked over at Lucy, who was holding a bright green child's toy phone in her hand. Lucy stared at it incredulously.

"What's this? I almost stepped on it on the floor,'' Lucy said.

"Car phone.''

"What?''

"Car phone. I read something once about how some people who can't afford regular car phones go out and buy fake ones as status symbols.''

"So you bought a kid's toy phone?" There was an over-tone of disgust in Lucy's voice.

"No. I bought the truck from Ryan." Ryan was the Delaney brother closest in age to Patricia and Maureen. Patricia wondered how long it had been since Maureen or Lucy had seen or talked to him, or any of the rest of the family. "His son left the toy in the truck, and when I asked Ryan about it he said not to bother returning it. James had outgrown it. I've just never gotten around to cleaning out the truck."

"No kidding. There's all kinds of shit on the floor." Lucy toed the littering of candy wrappers, a few pencils, a crumpled-up bag from an Arby's fast-food place.

Patricia shrugged. "My truck's the exception that proves the rule. I'm pain-in-the-ass neat everywhere else—just a warning. Still—don't you think that's kind of funny? A parody of a status symbol that's fake and totally useless. I've been tempted a few times when I'm bored in traffic to talk into it—see if I could get a reaction from other drivers."

The toy phone gave another ding as Lucy threw it back on the floor. "You're a weird chick, you know that?"

Patricia smiled. "Thanks. I figure that's a compliment from you."

She glanced over at Lucy and was glad to see her smiling with amusement. They had at least a temporary truce. Maybe the next three weeks would be long, but Patricia held out hope that they'd be at least somewhat enjoyable, too.

Patricia dangled an old sweat sock over Sammie's nose. He snapped it in his jaws, eager to play tug-of-war.

"Good boy—yeah. Get it! Get it!" Patricia said absently to her beagle, and yawned. She was lying on her couch in the small house she rented. She started to drift off, then was brought back by an insistent yank on the sock.

Patricia dropped her end of the sock. "Sorry, Sammie—I'm too pooped to be much fun now." Sammie stared up at her with sad, quizzical eyes, then proceeded to chew up the sock on his own.

Patricia got up and went into the kitchen to make her and

Lucy some sandwiches, smiling as she always did when she entered the cheery pale yellow kitchen.

Her home was the one thing in her life she had gotten by sheer luck, and Patricia normally didn't believe in either luck or fate. After setting up her business in Alliston, she commuted from her small apartment on the north side of the city. The drive wasn't that bad, but she started looking for a small house to rent. She had looked at a few places, but they were either too expensive or in a shambles.

One day she had been out driving through the countryside just for the pleasure of getting out of the city, when she came across this place with a "For Rent" sign out front. It was a former carriage house, on the premises of a five-acre estate that belonged to an accountant and a pediatrician, Joseph and Lina Carswell. They had converted the carriage house into a two-bedroom home for his mother. The mother had died recently, and they decided to rent it out rather than leave it empty, Patricia learned within the first few minutes of talking to Lina.

Patricia took it on the spot. The Carswells hadn't minded her doing a bit of redecorating. She left the wood floors bare, putting one large, deep red area rug beneath her blue-and-red-striped couch, coffee table, and white wicker rocker in the family room. She replaced the heavy drapes with deep red vertical blinds that matched the rug. Behind the couch was an antique floor lamp with a fringed white shade that had been her grandmother's. On either side of the patio door were large ficus trees.

One corner housed the television, CD player, and stereo equipment in an entertainment unit. Bookshelves and a desk filled one wall. By the gray stone fireplace in the opposite wall Patricia had her one piece of good art, a white abstract sculpture. Over the mantel was one of her own photographs, a black-and-white of sequoias viewed straight up from the ground, taken on a vacation to California.

Patricia had kept the two bedrooms and one bath the same. She slept in one bedroom and used the other to store her drums and extra books. She'd put an air mattress in there for Lucy, who was now in the room unpacking.

Outside, next to the patio, she grew a few flowers. Both she and Sammie were welcome to wander the five acres of woods freely, something she usually did at least once a weekend.

Patricia shut the refrigerator door. Without bread or mustard she couldn't make much of a sandwich.

She went over to her desk, picked up the phone to call in an order for Chinese takeout, then saw the red light blinking on her answering machine. She put back the receiver, pressed the message button, listened absently at first, then straightened up, alarmed, when she realized the urgency of the message.

It was from Elsa Kauffman, who half stuttered and cried while she tried to talk. "Patricia, it's me. Elsa Kauffman. They—they've found Andy. The police have just b-been here asking questions. They said they found him—his body—in a room at a motel in Kentucky. Dead."

Chapter 7

Upon the auctioneer's box Friedrich Kauffman was transformed. His chanted words arose from the middle of him, as if they were strings and he was the puppet, controlled by them even as he used them to control the crowd. His bright blue eyes scanned the crowd, seeking out and finding any twitch of eyebrow or finger or bidding card.

Under Friedrich's control the crowd was also transformed. It became a congregation of seekers for that special something, a congregation transfixed by Friedrich's eyes roaming, his finger pointing, his voice flexing just for a second, up a half note, then back to the chant, the words changing only slightly.

The process began with Friedrich holding each new item, perhaps something as ordinary as a chipped china cup, up to the crowd. But the way he held it with his one hand, the air still charged with the electricity of his previous calling for bids, made the cup seem like a holy chalice. The people in the crowd studied it, each person wondering, Is this it? Is this what I came here for? Is this that special something I've always wanted and never been quite able to identify?

Then Friedrich described the item reverently: "This is a fine bone-china cup with matching saucer, ladies and gentlemen. You won't find one like it in any store today, because it's nearly an antique—yessiree—genuu-wine Haviland china, with a pink rose, slight chip on the rim right here, but lovely, isn't it? Lovely in a cabinet with a collection. Lovely. I'll start the bidding at a dollar."

Then Friedrich's voice went off into the chant: "A dollar,

do I hear a dollar, a dollar—*yes*! Give me a dollar and a quarter, a quarter, ladies and gentlemen, for this fine china cup and sauce, a dollar and a quarter, a quarter—*yes*—and fifty—*yes*! Now give me . . ."

And the crowd's imagination was captured, its attention riveted on a china cup and saucer that had never known such rapt devotion and desire since the day it was first bought on sale at Elder's Department Store, fifty years before.

This was Friedrich's art, transforming a cup into a fine, fragile chalice that would bring beauty and charm to its possessor. Likewise his chant, as if it were derived from some ancient healing incantation, transformed him. He stood tall, the strings of his words pulling him up straight, his voice no longer sharp and demanding, but full and round.

Then the bidding slowed and stopped—a young woman with long blond hair, leggy in jeans, got the china cup and saucer for $2.50. The people around her watched her excitement, thinking, "What a bargain she got, I should have gone for $2.75, even $3.00. Why didn't I?"

And Friedrich stood on the auctioneer's box, smiling benevolently, looking over the crowd, his mind emptying of the need to focus on the china cup with the chip on the rim, ready to be transformed with the next item.

Patricia stood at the back of the crowd and, after the china cup sold, broke away and wandered off to the right of the farmhouse where the bigger items were displayed on the lawn for people to preview. They would be sold next, then finally the house.

Patricia wandered among the tables and chairs, china cabinets, and bed frames, looking around for Elsa. After listening to Elsa's phone message a second time, she called the Kauffman's business and home, but no one answered at either number. She remembered Elsa mentioning the auction, pulled the flier for it out of her briefcase, then headed out the door, leaving fifteen dollars for Lucy to call for pizza. Now she frowned, wondering where Elsa might be. Elsa had made it clear the day before that she intended to be here.

Before leaving for the auction, Patricia had called a friend with the police who not only confirmed that Andy Lawson had been found murdered in the motel, but added that he had been registered under the name of Jack Grierson. And that was the name of the man who had presumably bought the hatpins at Rosie's Attic, the hatpins that kept turning up at Friedrich's office with nasty notes skewered on them. So it was possible to imagine, thought Patricia, pausing to look at an old black-and-white gas stove, that Andy had been hiding out under this assumed name and delivering the hatpin notes at night. But that possibility brought up more questions than it answered.

Why would Andy send the notes in the first place? The notes had been vaguely threatening, but they didn't imply the bribery or extortion she would have expected from Andy. And why send the notes on these particular hatpins? What significance to the messages could they hold—for Andy or for Friedrich? The big questions, of course, were why was Andy murdered, and was his death related to the hatpins and their messages?

The last question sent a chill dancing across Patricia's skin, even on this hot and humid June day. She berated herself for developing theories she couldn't possibly defend without more information. She needed to find Elsa.

Patricia moved over to a dressing table to get out of the way of a couple who seemed seriously interested in the gas stove, and heard a familiar voice behind her. Turning around, she saw Brenda Gatts, Elsa's sister, standing by a china cabinet talking with an eager-looking young couple. Patricia moved closer to the edge of the little group.

"—Brookshire Estates lots, section five, have already sold! I'll tell you, honestly now"—Brenda leaned conspiratorially toward the couple like she was telling them something she wouldn't reveal to just anyone—"I've never seen lots sell like hot cakes like that before. It's just such an ideal location—"

"But thirty-five thousand for a quarter-acre lot—that seems like so much," the young woman said.

The man, slightly older and balding, frowned at her. "It is a prime location, dear," he said.

"True, true, and you're wise for noting the value of that. We have a saying in real estate—you can improve a lot about a house but not its location," Brenda said.

The man nodded wisely. The young woman glanced down at her loafers and didn't say anything.

"But I'll let you in on a little secret. I happen to know a developer is here today, and he is quite interested in this property for a future development—forty acres of prime development area. I'm sure he'll get it. A little farther out than Brookshire Estates, mind you, but—drive a little, save a lot. I like to tell my clients that! Now, here's my card—come see me when you want to see some lots!"

The man took the card eagerly and the young woman's face lit up, both apparently unaware that Brenda had just contradicted herself in her efforts to be their personal real-estate broker. They wandered off, talking excitedly with each other. Brenda shook her head.

"How about showing me a two-million-dollar mansion? My only requirement is an Olympic-size pool—"

Brenda jumped, turned, and stared at Patricia. Her expression went from eagerness to irritation to, finally, amusement. She laughed.

"Hi. I didn't see you."

"Sorry. I didn't mean to scare you. I've been standing here for a little while—you seemed pretty involved with the couple."

"Yeah, I guess. I always come out to the auctions—I'm Father's second voice, the only other trained auctioneer in our office. He always wants me in case he needs a break. He rarely does. Auctioneering is his number-one passion in life."

Patricia nodded. "I can see that." She could still hear Friedrich's voice over speakers set up in the yard. It was pervasive.

"So I always come, and try to meet a few people. I've picked up a few good clients that way," Brenda said.

"Like that couple?"

Brenda shook her head. "Ha. I know the type. They'll

come in to see me, insist on seeing all kinds of things they can't afford, then either get mad and leave, like it's my fault, or buy something overpriced that's only slightly better than where they are now. Either way a waste of time.''

Brenda smoothed a loose strand of hair back over her teased blond puff. Sweat had gathered on her upper lip. Even in the heat and humidity, she was in full makeup, drawn on in distinct, unblended lines in an attempt to camouflage extra weight and age lines: heavy brown eyebrows, bright aquamarine eyeshadow, thick mascara, a shock of peach on each cheek, and a matching shock of greasy peach lipstick on her mouth. She wore a low-cut green shirt and tight jeans that emphasized the extra padding on her hips. It was, thought Patricia, hard to believe she was Elsa's sister.

"I don't suppose you're here because you love auctions,'' Brenda was saying.

"No. I was hoping to find Elsa. She left me a message on my machine about Andy, and she told me yesterday about this auction. I wanted to see what I could find out—''

Brenda frowned. "Elsa. Elsa is useless. She's not here, although she is supposed to be helping out.'' Brenda smiled thinly. "I'm afraid my little sister is just so shaken up that she's at home in bed.''

"I tried calling the house—she must not be answering the phone.''

"That's not like her.'' A note of concern crept into Brenda's voice, and then she shrugged. "Who knows. Let's just say Elsa's not the kind you want around in an emergency.''

"Maybe you can help me, then.''

"Not much to tell. The police came this morning to the office. We were there having a pre-auction meeting. They talked to all of us briefly—but mostly to Father and Elsa. They said they would want to interview us each again at the station.''

"I learned that Andy was registered at a motel under a different name—a Jack Grierson.''

"Yes. Strange, isn't it? They wanted to know if we'd ever hired anyone by that name or if Andy had ever mentioned the name before. I'd never heard it. But he was registered under that name. Or someone he knew was, and he was visiting. But the motel owners insist they only saw one man go in and out of the room. The only way the police knew who he really was was because of his driver's license in his own name."

"Had Elsa heard the name before?"

"No. She was going to check the books later, see if the name appeared on any client lists. Or was possibly a temporary employee we'd forgotten about."

"Did the police mention how he was killed or where the motel was?"

"Strangled, I think. The motel was in northern Kentucky, not far across the river. Blue Bird Motel—something hokey like that." Brenda glanced at her watch and suddenly looked surprised. She looked around nervously.

"Maybe I could talk to your father after the auction. How long before this is over?"

"The house should go up in an hour, hour and a half. The bidding won't take too long after that."

"Are you looking for someone?" Patricia asked. Brenda was looking around more and more anxiously.

"Oh. I—" She looked at Patricia and grinned sheepishly. "Yes, Tom Nielson. He was supposed to get here a little early to discuss some business. Oh—there he is!" Brenda waved.

Patricia turned and saw Tom approaching. She remembered Brenda's comment to the couple that an "important developer" was going to be here today to buy the property. How could she know he'd get it? Then she remembered what she'd read in the articles she'd found with her computer; Friedrich had been accused once of planting auctions with his own bidders to buy up prime development property cheaply.

"Brenda, sorry I'm later than I said I'd be. My wife wanted me to drop her off at a friend's house before I came here."

The briefest look flickered across Brenda's face, but it expressed so much—irritation, jealousy, a tad of sadness. Patricia had a feeling that if she were working for Tom's wife to find out if Tom was fooling around, she'd end up outside Brenda's home one night, waiting to see what time of the morning Tom finally left.

Patricia cleared her throat. "Nice to see you again," she said. Tom looked at her vacantly.

"You met Patricia Delaney briefly at the office last week," Brenda explained. "She's a detective—doing some work for my father. She was trying to find Andy Lawson." Tom still looked blank.

Former football player made good, Patricia assessed, looking at Tom. At least good enough to sound prosperous at high-school and college reunions. He was handsome enough in a successful sort of way to be convincing—just the right touch of gray at the temples of his dark hair; firm, sensuous mouth; tall and well muscled. Unfortunately the vacantness of his hazel-gray eyes spoiled the effect. Whatever Brenda, or Friedrich, saw in him, it wasn't his brains.

"You may not remember me," Patricia said, allowing herself just the slightest smile. "As I recall you were rather angry—you had just stormed out of Friedrich Kauffman's office swearing you'd had enough and you weren't going to take it any more."

"Ah, yes. Now I remember." Tom laughed nervously. "Don't think anything of it Ms. . . . ."

"Just Patricia. Patricia Delaney."

"Patricia. Just one of those things in business—sometimes things can get a little tense when you're working on big projects together."

"My father tends to demand and get his own way," Brenda said. "A little frustrating for Tom, who's had so many successful projects on his own. Patricia, we'd like to stay and talk with you, but we have some business to discuss."

Patricia nodded. "I understand."

Tom and Brenda walked off together, disappearing behind the farmhouse.

Patricia passed the time by writing up some notes on the pad she always carried in her purse. Then she got a pair of greasy hot dogs and a Coke from a fast-food trailer set up by the edge of the road. The hot dogs settled into hard lumps in the bottom of her stomach, but at least they were something to eat, and the Coke was cold.

Finally it was time for the house and forty acres to go up for auction. Patricia stood at the back of the crowd, thinner now that all the small items and furnishings were gone. Brenda and Tom reappeared from behind the house, Tom taking a place up front, and Brenda just a few steps in front of Patricia.

Friedrich started the bidding at an incredibly low price. Tom was the first bidder. As Friedrich called the prices, raising them in small increments, he kept glancing back at Tom. The other bidders seemed impatient. Friedrich was no longer possessed by his art; he was working now. Sweat covered his face, and he was breathing hard.

In a remarkably short time he was about to end the bidding, but before he could cry "sold," another voice chimed in. "Three hundred and eighty thousand. Over here." Friedrich paused, frowning. That was fifty thousand more than the bid he had been prepared to accept. But he started the bidding again.

Patricia turned and found the man who had gotten the bidding going again. He was older, late sixties or early seventies, wearing bibbed overalls, white T-shirt, and a baseball cap. His features were thick and knobby: wide, bulbous nose; fleshy ears; baggy eyes. He chewed grimly on a hot dog between bids, his fleshy lips working laboriously around the food, his Adam's apple bobbing each time he swallowed.

Soon just Tom and the man were the only two bidding on the house. Tom hesitated to top the higher bids, but Friedrich kept nodding at him, glancing back at the man each time. Finally the man stopped bidding, once the price of the house and acreage had more than tripled the amount at which Friedrich had sought to stop the bidding.

Patricia looked back at the man. He had finished the hot dog and was wiping his mouth with the back of his hand. When his hand moved away, she saw the small, pleased grin on his face. Friedrich and the man know each other, Patricia thought. And the man knew he could get away with that. Friedrich would have cut off anyone else seeking to start up bidding again, but he had allowed this man to get away with it. And he had been determined for Tom to buy the house and land no matter what the price. Patricia was sure, instinctively, that this was true. What she didn't know, and wanted to, was why.

The man caught Patricia looking at him, and his grin dissolved. He turned and walked away quickly.

Patricia looked around for Brenda. She was moving up to the auctioneer's stand toward her father and Tom, who appeared to be having a heated conversation.

"Brenda," Patricia called.

Brenda stopped and turned. "Yes?"

"Who was that man? The one who started up the bidding again?"

Brenda hesitated, then said, "Leroy Hibberd. An acquaintance of Father's. He's a consultant to Father, although I'm not sure what he does. Something to do with the rental and office properties. Why?"

Patricia shrugged. "Just curious. He seemed anxious to get the house and land."

"I don't know about that. I do know Father is going to be furious. And so is Tom."

"I was hoping to speak to your father after the auction."

"I don't know if this is a good time, but then, who knows when a good time would be? Come on."

Patricia followed Brenda up to the auctioneer's stand, trying to place where she had seen or heard the name Leroy Hibberd before. And then she remembered. Mixed in with the articles about Friedrich's alleged practice of starting bidding low and ending it early with a plant to buy prime land had been a letter to the editor, written by Leroy Hibberd, with vague statements about past trouble for the Kauffman family.

Friedrich broke off immediately from Tom when he saw Brenda and Patricia approaching. "Brenda! What has taken you so long getting up here? We have enough work, especially without Elsa—'' He stopped and looked at Patricia, his eyes narrowing on her sharply. "You. If you had worked promptly, you could have found Andy and the money before he was murdered. Did Brenda tell you that when they found him, the money wasn't with him? Thieves. Always thieves.''

Then he stopped, turned, and walked away. Brenda and Tom followed him, without so much as a glance back at Patricia.

Patricia stood and watched Friedrich and his entourage walk away, then headed back to her truck. Friedrich had claimed to have no enemies, to be unable to fight. She was willing to bet that in the next few days she would learn differently.

Chapter 8

There was no Jack Grierson. At least there was no longer. Jack Grierson had died in the Vietnam War, in August 1965, while serving with an Explosive Ordnance Disposal unit in the army—an unfortunate accident. He had been five-seven, blond hair, blue-eyed. He died halfway around the world from his birthplace in Dayton, Ohio, when he was barely twenty-two; he had been born on July 5, 1943. Patricia wondered if his parents had secretly wished he had been born a day earlier just to be patriotic.

Tracking down this much information had been tedious work. First, Patricia had checked out the address "Jack" had given on the registry at Rosie's Attic. The address, Patricia learned from poring over property records for the city of Dayton, had once been a valid one. John and Alice Grierson had lived there for years, until the house had burned down and the land was rezoned commercial. From there, she checked into their property records, driving records, voting records, marriage license, and old articles from the *Dayton Daily News*. When she was all done, she learned that both the elder Griersons were dead, had only one child, Jack, who voluntarily entered the army at age twenty.

Somehow, somewhere along the way in his short life, Jack had known someone who would use his name as a cover for buying hatpins and registering in a Kentucky motel. That person had known him well enough to know his parents' old address. Patricia figured that the person had been with Jack in the military.

She'd contacted John Weaver, retired army colonel, at his

home in Washington, D.C. John was a close friend of her oldest brother, Joseph, who had also died in the Vietnam War, and still stayed in touch with her parents at holidays and intermittently throughout the year; he'd been a big part of why they had been able to heal, at least somewhat, from the loss of the oldest of their six children. Patricia knew that she could use the Freedom of Information Act to get copies of Jack's military records and a roster of the men he had served with through the National Personnel Records Center in D.C., but the truth was she didn't want to spend the time it would take without a little help from an old family friend.

John had promised he'd do his best, and now on her computer she saw a summary of what he had found in Jack's records. John, being a computer hobbyist, had sent her the message through an electronic bulletin board they both used, and added that official copies of the records were in the overnight mail to her. Finding the rosters of the companies in which Jack had served and getting them to her would be harder and take longer, but he would do it.

Patricia reread the message, saved it on her computer, and printed it out for the *Kauffman, hatpins* file.

With a host of databases at her disposal thanks to her computer, Patricia could pull together all kinds of information. She could tap into everything from newspapers and magazines and newsletters to all the records publicly held companies have to file with government agencies in order to even exist. Other databases let her take a look at larger private companies. State statutes and cases, case law, criminal records, motor-vehicle or pleasure-boat and aircraft registrations . . . any kind of public record was available to her, most of them through her computer. There were even databases of scientific and academic papers, useful when she was checking out potential candidates for jobs at Alliston College, as she was doing now on a different case. An electronic bulletin board just for licensed investigators let her get, and give, help to other investigators across the country without ever leaving her desk.

What her computer could not do for her was figure out

who might have known Jack Grierson long ago and want to use his name now to buy hatpins and make motel reservations. She'd have to rely, to some degree, on Weaver's help for that, but she had some other places to look herself. She finished off her glass of iced coffee, not relishing the need to venture out into the heavy, humid day with temperatures in the upper nineties. But she knew where she needed to go next. Patricia grabbed her briefcase and headed for the door, on her way to the Blue Bird Motel.

The young man looked seventeen, maybe eighteen. He was trying to look older, thus the peach-fuzz mustache and frown. He was also trying to look tough. His long blond hair grazed his shoulders and he wore a black shirt with a black tie and stonewashed black jeans. He was scowling into a magazine, which had a fancy race car on the cover, and sat behind the counter, his feet propped up on a desk. Lucy's type, Patricia thought.

The young man was doing a good job of not noticing her; Patricia had been standing in the lobby, really a small square of worn and dirty tile, for a full two minutes. She used the time to size him up before she started asking questions.

The police had already been to the Blue Bird Motel, of course, and most people would be reluctant to answer the same questions the police had asked, even for a licensed private investigator. But if this kid was Lucy's type, he probably hated cops, and she could use that to her advantage. She swatted the bell on the counter.

He jumped, nearly falling back in his half-tilted chair, fumbled with the magazine, finally righted himself, and stood, scowling down at her. He was a good six feet four inches, but the way he held himself indicated he lacked the grace or experience of an athlete. The scowl, she figured, came in part from the young man being asked too many times why he wasn't a basketball player. He wore a name tag that said *Larry Robbins*.

"Yeah? What room are you checking out of?"

"I'm not checking out."

"Okay. It's earlier than people usually check in, but I'll tell you what we got—clean enough rooms, single for twenty-one dollars, double for twenty-three-fifty, one water-bed suite for thirty-five, no room service, but there's vending machines around the corner of this building and a restaurant across the way that's open twenty-four hours. I recommend the vending machines, myself, except for coffee. So what'll it be?"

"I'm not checking in, either," Patricia said.

"What, you're meeting someone here?" Larry smiled, widened his eyes, and licked the bottom of his top row of teeth. "Do you happen to know his name, or should I give you a list of our current guests?"

Patricia withheld a laugh. Larry was Lucy's type—rebellious and irreverent. Witty. Patricia liked that. She worried about kids who were too well behaved.

"Not today, thanks. Maybe you could answer a few questions for me about Andy Lawson. Checked in as Jack Grierson. Murdered in Room 212, I believe, and you found the body." She had learned that much, from a second call to her police friend, who she had met at Adam's Security and Investigations and who now worked on the Cincinnati police force and had connections throughout Ohio, Indiana, and Kentucky.

The scowl remained on Larry's face, but now he licked his lips nervously.

"Look—I answered all your people's questions yesterday. I don't know anything more than what I already told you." He thought she was police, and normally Patricia would have let him keep thinking it if it would make him talk with her more openly. In this case it would only work against her. Patricia frowned as if she were annoyed.

"You don't think I'm a cop, do you? Please!" She half laughed, half snorted as if she were disgusted. "I'm Patricia Delaney, a private investigator." She pulled a business card out of her pocket and snapped it against the countertop. "I've got my own questions to ask for a client of mine."

Larry picked up the card and inspected it closely. It always amazed Patricia how many people saw a business card as proof of her legitimate right to ask questions. She carried a copy of her license for anyone who asked to see it; few did.

Satisfied, Larry gave the card back to Patricia. She tucked it in her purse, then leaned forward, looked worried, and said conspiratorially, "Look, could you do me a favor? If the cops come sniffing around here, don't tell them I've been by asking my own questions. They like to think they're the only ones who can ask anyone anything."

Larry grinned suddenly, happy to be a co-conspirator against authority, and said, "Yeah. I've heard cops don't like you private eyes."

"What can you tell me about Andy Lawson?"

"Not much, except he was kind of a strange guy. I mean, besides the fact that he checked in under a false name. I work the later hours, after school until about eight o'clock when my mom takes over again. I usually see people check in, come in and ask a question, directions or something to wherever they're going—no one comes here just for being here, you know what I mean? This is just a cheap stopping place off the highway on the way to Lexington or somewhere else.

"But this guy—he reserved the room by phone in advance, for two weeks," Larry continued. "And he always stuck to himself—usually kept the 'Do Not Disturb' sign out and said when he checked in that he didn't want maid service unless he took that sign down, which was about every other day."

"He told you that when he checked in?"

"Not me, my dad."

"Your dad checked him in."

"Yeah."

"So you didn't see him at all until after he'd been here what, a night or two?"

"Probably two nights, but what does that matter? I saw him after that."

Patricia shrugged. "Just trying to get my facts straight. So you saw him later—"

"Yeah."

"What did he look like?"

Larry thought about that one. "Hard to say, really. That was sort of weird, too. He wore a hat pulled down on his head, so you couldn't really see his hair, and a blue sweat suit with the collar turned up. Made you think maybe he was bald and trying to hide it. And he always had on these big dark sunglasses, hid half of his face. Always had on the same blue sweat suit. First time I got a good look at him was when I found him. Dead."

"Any facial hair, scars, that kind of thing?"

"Nope."

"How tall was he?"

"Probably five-eight. No, a little taller, probably. I always think people are shorter than they really are."

"Medium build?"

"Yeah, I guess so. He always wore the same blue sweat suit, kind of too big for him. It was hard to tell. 'Cept I remember thinking—later, not at the time—when I found him that he seemed skinnier than I would have thought."

"Was he wearing the hat, or sunglasses, or sweat suit when you found him?"

Larry frowned. "No. He was in jeans and a T-shirt and boots. No hat or sunglasses. He had blond hair."

"Was he younger or older than you expected?"

"Younger. He'd always kind of shuffled around before."

"When you did see him around, what was he doing?"

"Crossing to the greasy spoon across the way, maybe getting something from the vending machine. He was only out every other day or so."

"What kind of car did he drive?"

"That was kind of strange, too. There was no license number on his registration form, and no car parked in front of his motel room. It's like he hitchhiked or walked here or something."

"Did he use a credit card when he reserved the room?"

Larry shook his head. "Sent us cash, with a typed note that just had his name and the dates he would be staying. Paid the rest of the bill up front in cash, too. Most people use credit cards these days."

"Do you mind if I take a look at his registration form?"

Larry hesitated. "I don't know. . . . ."

Patricia smiled conspiratorially. "C'mon. I need the information to help out my client, you know?"

Larry grinned slowly. First he had found the dead body, now he was helping a lady private eye pull off a hot case behind the cops' backs. That could really help the status of a too-tall kid with no talent for basketball in a small high school. He found the registration form and handed it over to Patricia.

It was filled out in the same block letters that had been used to fill out the guest book at Rosie's Attic. The same obsolete address was listed. Patricia handed back the form. It gave a check-in time in a different handwriting, presumably Larry's father's, but no checkout date or time.

"Thanks. What made you look in his room?"

"Sally, one of the maids—she works here after school, too—came and told me he'd had the 'Do Not Disturb' sign up for three days in a row, and none of us had seen him around. I looked on the form, and as you saw, it hadn't been marked that he'd checked out early or anything. So I thought I'd better look into it. My mom was off doing errands. My dad—he was wherever he goes. So I went to the door of Room 212.

"Well, I knocked, and he didn't answer," Larry continued. "So I knocked a few more times and called his name, but no answer. Then Sally looked anxious and said, maybe he's sick, maybe we should call an ambulance or the cops or something."

Larry paused to scowl. "But who needs them, right? So I kicked the door open, just like I've seen it done on TV."

"Just like that?"

Larry looked a little sheepish, then quickly resumed his proud stance. "It's harder than it looks. But after a few good kicks I got the door open. And that's when I found him."

"Dead."

"Yeah. At first I thought he was just sleeping, stretched out on the bed. I walked over, saying 'Mr. Grierson,' but got no answer. Then I flicked on a light and looked at him, and realized he was dead. Strangled. A bandanna was still around his neck, and he was tied up, his hands to the bed-post, and gagged with pieces of a ripped-up sheet. Looked like he'd also been hit over the head. His wrists were bruised like he'd struggled. The cops said he'd been dead over a day." Larry looked a little sick to his stomach at that.

"Why do you think he was here?"

"Beats me. Most people, like I said, stay one night on the way to somewhere more interesting—that'd be about any-where—and that's it. There's nothing much in town—a dinky hospital, few bars, shops, churches. Regular stuff, no mu-seums or anything that would draw anyone. Further down the highway is a nice state park. Sometimes we get some spillover from the towns down there, but it's been too hot this summer."

"You didn't see anybody—a little shady—coming by reg-ularly? To see him?"

Larry frowned and shook his head. "My parents run a clean place. No drugs or hookers."

Patricia glanced around the tiny lobby like she was seeing it for the first time. "Your parents own it," she said. "Nice."

Larry shrugged. "It's their dream, not mine. I'm out of this hole-in-the-wall town as soon as I graduate next year." He said it with just the right mix of defiance and desperation in his voice for Patricia to know that he was afraid of some-thing or someone holding him back—his parents? Or maybe Sally the maid? Or just fear. She wanted to wish him luck but figured he wouldn't want to hear it—he didn't need luck, right?

"You said your dad checked Jack in. Can I see your dad?"

"Sure. He's not here now, but you might catch him at the greasy spoon across the way. That's where he was going when I got here." Larry resumed his disgusted scowl. "Don't know why. The place'll make you puke. I wouldn't take any chances with what they serve."

Patricia grinned. "Thanks for the tip."

"Sure."

"And thanks for helping me out. And, uh, if you could not tell the cops I was here if they come back around . . ."

The happily conspiratorial grin was back on Larry's face. "You bet!"

Patricia left and crossed the street to the Lucky Clover Diner. The minute she was inside, she saw why Larry didn't like the place, and it had nothing to do with the decor or the food. The diner was decorated nicely in green and white, as befitted the name, with green-and-white-checked table-cloths, a spring-green color on the walls, and a border of white with green four-leaf clovers. The smell of fresh coffee and a display of cakes and pies above the counter were tempting. It reminded Patricia that she'd just had coffee for breakfast, and it was well past lunchtime.

Patricia was the only one in the place with the exception of a man—very tall, with a shock of blond hair just like Larry's except it was cut short. He had to be Larry's father. He sat on a stool at the counter, and a woman, a waitress in a green waitress's short-sleeved dress with a frilly little white apron, sat in his lap, giggling and tugging at his baseball cap. That explained why Larry didn't like the place.

The waitress finally noticed her, hopped down, grabbed a menu from the counter, and approached Patricia. Larry's father went back to his coffee and newspaper.

"Follow me," she said. Her name was Betty, according to the name patch on her dress.

"I don't need a menu—just coffee. And I believe I'm here to see this gentleman," Patricia said. A sandwich or salad would be good, but she was on business; she'd stop for something on the way back to Cincinnati. She went over to Larry's father and hopped up on the stool next to him. He kept looking at his paper, ignoring her.

"Are you Mr. Robbins?"

He didn't look up. Betty appeared behind the counter, put a coffee mug in front of Patricia, poured her coffee. Then she looked at the man and said, "Need a warm-up, Earl?"

He looked up at Betty and smiled. "Yeah, thanks," he

said. He looked over at Patricia slowly. His expression was more weary than anything else. "Did you want something?"

"My name's Patricia Delaney, and I'm a private investigator. I have a client who was involved with Andy Lawson—registered at your motel as Jack Grierson. I was just over at your motel, talking with your son, and he mentioned you were the one who'd signed Andy in. I want to ask you a few questions."

Earl just kept looking at her. Betty leaned on the counter and took Earl's hand. They were waiting for her to leave. Maybe she'd stumbled on the one time a week in daylight hours they could be together. Patricia shrugged and tossed a dollar on the counter. She started to leave.

"Never mind, Earl," she said. "I'll just talk to your wife. I'll tell her the two of you said hi."

"No—wait," Earl said. Patricia settled back down on the stool. Betty hurried back to the kitchen.

Earl smiled sheepishly. "I—I was just trying to recollect the man."

"Shouldn't be too hard to recall a man who stayed at your motel and got murdered in his room."

Earl shrugged. "I only saw him when he checked in, then around a few times. He was alone—stuck to himself. Wasn't the chatty type."

"Did he mention why he was here?"

Earl shook his head. "Nope."

"Why do you think he was here—if you had to guess."

Earl finished off his coffee and stared into the empty cup before he answered.

"People around here make their living farming, or working at the places by the highway for the truckers and travelers passing through. That's the only reason he'd be here. Passing through."

"You don't pass through by staying for two weeks. Maybe he was visiting someone around here."

Another shake of the head. "I'd have heard of it by now. People around here are like coon dogs, sniffing out other people's business. It's their entertainment."

Earl, Patricia thought, had been burned a time or two by that. "So you never saw anyone come to his room or saw him talk to anyone. Did anyone who works for you mention seeing him talk with anyone?"

"No . . ." Earl paused, thinking. "Now wait. I did see him once in here, talking with Randy."

"Randy?"

"Randy Finster. Trucker that's got a regular route through here. Betty! Hey, Betty!" Betty barged immediately through the swinging doors from the kitchen. She had, Patricia realized, been just inside the doors listening to every word.

"Betty, this here lady—"

"Patricia Delaney."

"She's doing some investigating for a friend of that man who was murdered over at the motel."

Betty made a face, scrunching her mouth up in disgust. She and Earl will never sleep in that room again, thought Patricia.

"I told her I'd seen him in here once talking with Randy Finster."

"Oh—yes," said Betty. "They got to talking over by the arcade games."

"When would that have been?" Patricia asked.

Betty thought a minute. "Monday last, had to be. Randy has a regular route through here, Mondays and Thursdays. Always stops in. Gets dinner."

"About what time?"

"Evenings. Seven o'clock."

"Was that the only time you saw them talking?"

"Hmm. No—saw them again last Thursday."

Patricia calculated in her mind. That would have been the day before Andy was found in the room. "Did you happen to hear anything they were saying?"

Betty frowned, looking offended at the thought. "No. I don't listen to my customers' conversations."

Patricia grinned. "Good idea. Thanks for your help," she said, leaving two dollars on the counter. That more than covered the coffee and service. But then, she wanted to leave

Betty and Earl in a good mood. She'd be back to talk with the trucker, and she didn't want them to tell him anything that might keep him from talking.

Chapter 9

It was after dinner in the Kauffman household, and Elsa and Friedrich sat in the family room silently. Friedrich was in his chair, reading about World War I. Elsa sat on the couch, looking at her romance novel without really reading it. Elsa put the book down, finally, and looked over at her father.

They had not spoken all through dinner, except when he asked her to pass him something. They had barely spoken before dinner. And, thought Elsa, they could go all the rest of the evening without speaking. The silence pressed down on her, a suffocating, stifling weight.

She thought about Andy Lawson. Andy had been one of the favorites in the office, at least with her father. Friedrich had seen him as smart, assertive, motivated. The others liked him, or pretended to, because Friedrich did.

Elsa had been uncomfortable with Andy, partly because he stopped by her desk when no one else was around, and made jokes that she didn't get, but that she suspected were nasty. He always had a kind of sneer around his mouth at those times, and he seemed to take pleasure in the fact that she could only respond with a weak smile. But he was perfectly polite to her when her father, or others, were around.

The other reason he made her uncomfortable was because of how he looked—slim, blond, blue eyes. His looks reminded her of a boy, Kent, that she had liked in high school, except that the thinness in Andy's mouth seemed to indicate cruelty, whereas in Kent it just seemed a sign of vulnerability.

"Elsa—more iced tea! Aren't you listening?"

Elsa put aside her book, got her father's glass, went back to the kitchen, and brought it out again, refilled with iced tea. She sat back down on the end of the couch, reached for her own glass, and realized it was empty. She started to the kitchen again, but her father's voice stopped her.

"Where was your mind?"

"I was thinking about—about Andy. How sad it is."

"Oh. Yes." Friedrich started reading again.

Leave it alone, she thought, knowing it would be best to go back to her book, to try to get lost in the fantasy it provided. But she didn't want to go back to the silence just yet.

"I wonder if we should call Kurt," Elsa said.

"He's on vacation. He'll find out soon enough when he's back day after tomorrow."

"But he may want to help with the—the service." The Kauffmans were organizing a memorial service. The actual funeral would be in Utah.

Friedrich looked up at her, frowning. "I hadn't realized they were that close." If they were, he'd want to know about it. Friedrich jealously monitored all relationships around him.

"They weren't. Close, I mean. It's just that working together and all—"

"They shared the same desk." Friedrich said, dismissing the conversation with a clipped tone and returning to his book.

Elsa persisted, knowing she shouldn't, knowing she would invoke her father's wrath, and an anger in herself that ultimately would die unexpressed. She was like a driver intent on crashing into a wall for the sake of feeling something.

"Will we start looking for another agent soon?"

"A week will be soon enough."

"I wonder if Patricia will find who killed Andy. I think she will—she just—"

Friedrich closed his book and slammed it down on the table next to him. "For God's sake, Elsa. What is it you want?"

"I just thought—I just thought—I—" The words were

stuck in her throat, and her shoulders started quaking. The rage had control of her now. It only arose every now and then, but when it did, it choked her inexplicably, it convulsed her body. It combusted inside of her, consuming energy and thought internally, but was never directed at anyone.

Elsa hunched forward, shaking, hugging herself, rocking back and forth, her mouth gaping silently, a thin line of spittle trickling from its corner. And then suddenly she stopped rocking. She still shook, but less. She closed her mouth and rubbed the back of her hand across it.

"I just thought we—we—we—" She stopped and swallowed. She wanted a sip of her tea, then realized again that her glass was empty. It did not occur to her to ask for a sip of her father's tea, or to him to offer it.

"I just thought we should talk about what happened to Andy. I mean, he's dead and shouldn't we—"

"We're all sorry he's dead, Elsa. What else is there to discuss?"

Elsa's mouth gaped once, then clenched shut.

Friedrich smiled at her. "Good. I'm glad you have calmed down. Now, I want you to fire—what is that detective's name—Delaney. Fire her tomorrow."

"Fire—fire Patricia?"

"You heard me. She wasn't any help, and I didn't like her attitude. Too probing. Now that Andy's dead, we don't need her."

Friedrich went back to his book. Elsa slumped in the couch. She was no longer enraged, but was exhausted, hollowed out from the impotent anger that had flared and died within her.

Thought returned to her slowly. Her father wanted her to fire Patricia. She wouldn't do it. She was surprised and pleased at the same time at her sudden stubbornness. The last time she had been defiant had been with Kent, when they had skipped school together to go to the old Coney Island park in Cincinnati on the Ohio River, to ride the rides and eat popcorn and cotton candy and laugh until they were both exhausted.

She wouldn't fire Patricia. She'd keep her on, just not let her father know, and she wouldn't let Patricia know that her father had asked her to fire her. She'd pay her out of her own savings if necessary, or see if she could juggle the books. She hated to tamper with the books, but she knew how to do it. Her father had told her to do it more than a few times before.

Elsa needed Patricia, not just to find some answers for her, but because Patricia was strong. Elsa had a glimmering of hope that if she was around Patricia enough she'd find a defiance in herself she'd never manage alone, and escape from the meaninglessness of her life.

But for now, something less grand would have to distract her. She glanced at her book, but it had lost its appeal.

The pictures. She had rediscovered the pictures and scrapbooks and letters of her grandmother Gertrude Kauffman. She had just started going through them. Elsa stood up slowly and started quietly up the stairs to the attic.

Friedrich listened to Elsa's footsteps going out of the room and up the stairs. When he was satisfied that she was gone, he put his book down. He rubbed his eyes hard, sat quietly for a moment, then slowly let the thoughts and feelings in. He was too tired to hold them back, and Elsa's fit brought them forth.

The first time he had seen her shake with silent rage had been that night, years and years ago when Elsa was just a little girl. She had been the apple of his eye until then—so ready to laugh, so spontaneous and smart and pretty.

His wife had claimed Brenda and Henry as her own, withdrawing with them from him. By the time Elsa was born, she had been satisfied to withdraw with just her undiagnosable, unnamed aches and pains. She didn't have much time for Elsa. Perhaps because of that, Elsa turned to him. Something in him must have delighted Elsa, because nothing could make her face light up like a hug and a kiss from her papa. She accepted him fully, and she was the first and only person ever to do so.

But then came that night, when he came home late, filthy

and terrified out of his mind from an act so reprehensible he had pushed it immediately into a back room in his mind, determined to forget it. And he could have—he would have—if Leroy Hibberd hadn't come to him later. But the biggest reminder throughout his life had always been the look of fear in Elsa's eyes.

Elsa had been unable to sleep that night. So, naturally, when she heard his footsteps coming in, she slipped out of bed, anxious to greet him. He remembered all too well her reaction when she saw him. She saw the terror and guilt on his face, although she was too young to name them as such. She recoiled from him, disappointed and dismayed, as so many others had recoiled from him. Something in him snapped for a second time that night, and he smacked her across the face. That was the first time he saw the rage build up in her, making her shake. Then he grabbed her by the arms and told her to stay quiet. Her little mouth had gaped, opening and shutting like she was trying to breathe great gulps of air. He told her to go back to her bed and not tell anyone she'd seen him, or she'd really be in trouble.

After that she became a sullen, pensive child, withdrawing from him, and that made him angry over and over again with her, because every time he looked at her he saw how he failed the one person who had loved and accepted him for himself. He wanted to be strong and confident, pushing back fear, trying to be like the father he could not remember, but that his mother always told him about. He wanted to overcome the dismay and pity he saw in people's faces when they realized he had one arm and a crippled leg, and be, in spirit at least, like his father, who loomed in his mind strong, and tall, and whole, and unconquerable.

The struggle to live up to that image had made him hate weakness and fear in himself and in others. When he sensed it in others, he wanted to destroy it, like an animal who senses fear in another animal and instinctively is incensed to attack.

And since that night he had sensed fear in Elsa. Her cowering and lack of confidence enraged him, yet he knew that he was partly responsible for it, planting the seed that night and later reinforcing it with anger.

Foolish. He was foolish for indulging in all this self-analysis. None of it mattered now—his guilty secrets were just that, for he had paid dearly to make sure those secrets would go with him to the grave; any mistakes he had made had only been made because he'd been pushed by circumstances he couldn't control. No one could blame him for that. No one could. He opened his book and began reading again about the World War I heroes, none of whom, Friedrich was sure, had displayed the courage of his own father.

Chapter 10

Lucy came bounding in through the back patio door with Sammie.

"Wow! What a great place! The woods back there are beautiful. We must have hiked—" She stopped, finally noticing Patricia's odd position. She sat in the lotus position on the floor, left hand palm up on her knee, while holding her right nostril closed with her right index finger. She took long, deep, slow breaths.

"What the hell are you doing?" Lucy demanded. She released Sammie from his leash, and he trotted up to Patricia and sat down quietly at her right knee.

For a few seconds Patricia didn't respond. Then she opened her eyes slowly. When Sammie saw that his master was back in his world again, he pounced on her lap and started licking her face.

Patricia laughed, rubbed Sammie behind the ears, and looked up at Lucy. "Meditating. Breathing exercises. Good for the soul. Kind of like spiritual flossing. I recommend it at least once a day."

"You're kidding."

"No, I'm not. And you're only forgiven once for interrupting. I'll be glad to teach you the techniques."

"Uh, thanks. Maybe some other time."

"Fine." Patricia unfolded herself, gave Sammie a final scratch, then went to the CD player. She put on a CD. "You were saying something when you came in."

"Oh, yeah. The woods behind here. They're neat. Sammie and I probably spent two hours hiking around back there.''

"Then you're probably hungry." Patricia started back to the kitchen. "Don't come in here just yet, until I call for you."

A few minutes later Patricia called for Lucy to come to the kitchen. She smiled as the girl came bounding in, then stopped, her eyes widening when she saw what was on the small kitchen table: cheese soufflé, asparagus in hollandaise sauce, a spinach salad, crusty home-baked bread, and waiting on the counter for dessert, a white chocolate mousse cake.

"Wow," said Lucy. "You made all this?"

"With my own little hands." Patricia had come home early from her office to prepare the meal.

"Mom told me you said you weren't Betty Crocker, basically to fend for myself with sandwiches."

"Mostly that's true. Every now and then I like to do something special in the kitchen. Don't want my skills to get too rusty."

Lucy looked at Patricia wryly. "Let me guess. At one point in your life you were a gourmet chef for a cruise ship. . . ."

Patricia laughed. "Not exactly. I dated a guy for a while who was a gourmet chef. Unfortunately the only thing in my life he heated up was my kitchen. But I got a few good tips and recipes from him." She paused and smiled at Lucy gently. So far their visit had gone smoothly. Lucy had dropped the tough-stuff front, and sensitive subjects—like her problems with the law and her mother—hadn't come up again. "Happy seventeenth, kiddo."

"You knew it was my birthday?"

"I was there when you were born, telling Maureen to breathe. I'm not likely to forget it," Patricia said, and then immediately wished she hadn't. She suspected from the glimmer of sadness in Lucy's eyes that Maureen had forgotten. Call tonight, Maureen, thought Patricia, and wish your kid a happy birthday.

"Thanks, Patricia."

"Sure. C'mon, let's dig in."

The two women sat down and started eating, talking only occasionally, about the weather, the news, Sammie, how Patricia had come to find her place.

At the end of the meal Lucy said, "That was great! I don't know about meditating, but you can teach me what you know about cooking if you want."

"Thanks. Maybe I will. Got room for white chocolate mousse cake?"

"You bet."

"Okay. Let's get these dishes cleared away first."

Patricia cleared dishes while Lucy rinsed them and stacked them in the small dishwasher.

"What was that music playing through dinner?" Lucy asked.

"*La Traviata*. My favorite opera, so don't say anything."

"It was okay. I've never really listened to opera before."

"It's like meditating or cooking or anything else. You have to give it a chance."

"I don't get it. You listen to opera, but you play drums in a rock band, and you studied violin in college for a while. At least that's what Mom said."

"She was right," Patricia said. "What, you think my eclectic taste in music is strange?"

"Unusual, anyway."

Patricia and Lucy returned to the table, each with a plate of cake.

"I guess my musical tastes are unusual. Father was a school music teacher. Always wanted to be a singer, though," Patricia said. "He loved the opera. That's where my love for opera and the violin come in. I guess I showed a talent for music at a young age—you'd have to ask him how—at least more so than the other kids, and he kind of latched onto that. Dragged me off to every opera he possibly could. Gave me music lessons—piano, flute, violin . . . I was decent enough at the violin, and I liked it enough, that I did study violin for a while in college here, at the Conservatory of Music. That's how I first came to this city."

Patricia smiled at the memory. "I played a little guitar, but mostly drums in a rock band as a teenager, partially for the fun of it, and partially because it drove my dad nuts. To him, I wasn't taking violin seriously enough if I was also banging around like an ape, as he liked to put it. He was probably right."

"It's hard to imagine you playing in a rock band then, or now," Lucy said.

Patricia laughed. "Do I look that conventional?"

Lucy grinned. "Well, yeah. But I guess if you were a club dancer . . ."

"Oh, my checkered past coming back to haunt me."

Lucy laughed, and Patricia was glad to hear the laugh was genuine, gleeful, almost a giggle. Behind the stark makeup and shock hair, she was just a teenager looking for direction, Patricia thought. Too bad Maureen was too enmeshed in her own problems to provide some guidance.

"I play guitar in a band, too," Lucy said.

Patricia nodded. "That's what your mom said." At that Lucy looked uncomfortable. Oops, thought Patricia, let's get back to safe territory. "We'll dig mine out of the closet in your room tomorrow. I'm not sure of its condition now, but you can play it if you want."

"Thanks," said Lucy. She poked a piece of cake around with her fork, then looked back up at Patricia. "Why didn't you stick to it? The violin, I mean? If you were good enough to get in the conservatory here . . ."

"That was Dad's dream for me, not mine," Patricia said.

"What was yours?"

"Can't say I specifically had one, except I knew when I watched the other kids at college, so serious, so in love with their music, I knew that wasn't for me. I liked playing, I liked the atmosphere, but I just couldn't see me practicing, struggling, every day for the rest of my life to play a violin moderately well for a symphony somewhere."

"So what did you do then?" Lucy asked. She finished off her piece of white chocolate mousse cake and settled back in her chair.

"Dropped out of school at the end of the first year. Enrolled in the University of Cincinnati for the summer term, instead of going home to teach violin to little kids like I was supposed to, then called my parents and told them what I had done. Not the nicest way to handle it, but I was terrified about what my parents—especially my dad—would do."

Lucy laughed. "Gramps probably went through the roof."

"Yes. He cut me off, at least temporarily. I got the job at Poppy's Parrot and somehow got through the summer. By fall, Dad saw I was serious, that I wasn't going to be a musician. He helped me out, somewhat begrudgingly, and I double-majored in history and English simply because they were subjects I'd liked in high school."

Lucy looked down at her empty plate and then turned it in slow circles on the table. "Sounds like you and Gramps were pretty close. I mean, he stuck by you in the long run."

Patricia sucked in her breath sharply. She had a feeling they had just moved into territory she wasn't fully prepared to deal with. She wasn't used to being around teenagers, especially ones looking for some guidance. Dammit, why couldn't Maureen pay attention to her kid?

"Yes," said Patricia. "Dad and I are pretty close, although we're enough alike that we can rub each other the wrong way. Mom and I are different from one another, and she also can't understand why I like the line of work I'm in, but we're close, too. Always have been."

"Gee, sounds great. Ideal family."

"Don't get sarcastic on me, Lucy. Not ideal. Nobody's family is ideal."

Lucy sighed. "Yeah, I know. But it sounds nice."

"It is."

"What was Mom like?" Lucy asked. "I mean when she was a kid."

"Oh, rebellious, I guess. I was, too, but she was kind of—wild about it. Fun loving. Pretty. Kind, when she wanted to be. I always thought she was so—invincible—but then . . ." Patricia sighed. "I don't know, Lucy, if you want me to be honest about your mother, I guess I'd have to say she always had a penchant for getting into trouble. I'm not sure why. Nobody's sure why. She never seemed to focus on one thing very long, at least not long enough to find out if she was any good at it.''

"Like now," Lucy said softly. She looked up at Patricia, her eyes shimmering behind tears. "Like me.''

"Whoa, kiddo. You're you. Not a copy of your mother. You've got to live your own life, not spend it reacting to what others around you are doing.''

"Like by stealing stuff, you mean," Lucy said. A bit of the old smirk passed across her face, then disappeared.

"Okay. Like by stealing stuff. Or whatever.''

Lucy looked away from Patricia, turning something over in her mind. Patricia waited, quietly, for her to speak. Then Lucy looked back at her, almost defiantly.

"I'm thinking of leaving home, living with a friend in the fall.'' At Patricia's alarmed look Lucy laughed. "Don't worry, it's not one of the kids I got into trouble with. A friend from the band. She said she'd check with her parents, see what they'd say. I don't know, I guess I think if I could get away from Mom's problems, think for a while, I could figure out what to do with my life. What do you think?''

Patricia considered. She knew what Maureen would want her to say, for all her problems she tended to see Lucy as an anchor, someone to turn back to when the latest guy ran out on her.

Patricia took a deep breath, exhaled it slowly. "I think it might be a good idea. But you have to decide for yourself.''

"You don't give answers, do you?" Lucy suddenly looked angry. "I mean, everyone else seems to have an answer for me—like, Mom wants me to stay out of trouble, and out of sight when one of her guys is around. My boyfriend wants me to run off with him to New York next year. My counselor thinks I'm smart and oughta go for a college scholarship somewhere. But you won't say what you think.''

"I just said what I think. You've got to decide for yourself.'' Patricia reached over and covered Lucy's hand with hers. "Look, you want some advice from Auntie Patricia?''

"Yeah, sure."

"Okay, here's the best I can do. I wish I could say I have no regrets about quitting the violin. But sometimes I wonder if my dad was right, if playing the violin would have been the best life for me. Most of the time I'm glad for the life I've lived so far. I love my work, I'm independent, and that's always been the biggest thing to me. And I still get lost in playing the drums from time to time. But I can't say no regrets."

"No easy answers in life, right?"

Patricia smiled, removed her hand from Lucy's, and leaned back in her chair.

"Right. But whatever you choose—make sure it's you choosing it. Okay?"

Lucy smiled. "Okay. Thanks, Patricia."

"Sure. We can talk again later, if you want. But I've got to go meet a client in a few minutes. Clear up the rest of the dishes for me?"

Lucy nodded and went straight to work.

Patricia went back to her bedroom, to change out of her jeans and T-shirt into a pair of casual pants and blouse. She was going to meet Elsa Kauffman at the agency office. Patricia had called her earlier that day, asking her to check for any references to a Jack Grierson in her employee or client files. Elsa had agreed, and said she wanted to meet her, but after hours at the office, saying they were swamped. It seemed strange, but then, thought Patricia as she rummaged through her jewelry box for a pair of earrings, there wasn't much about this case that was ordinary.

She found the earrings she wanted, but then she paused, frowning. Something seemed out of place. Her jewelry collection was small and simple; she had no pieces that were of particular value, except one. It was a gold necklace, with a small treble clef set with a tiny diamond. She rarely wore it. It had been given to her by a young man she had known and loved very much while at the Cincinnati Conservatory. Their planned life together had not worked out, but she had always kept the necklace as a reminder of the time they had shared.

It always gave her a tiny jolt in her heart to see it, but whenever she opened the small jewelry box, her eyes automatically darted to it.

And now it was missing.

Patricia squeezed her eyes shut, clenched her teeth. There had to be an explanation for it, other than the one that instantly came to mind. She couldn't believe—at least, she didn't want to believe—that Lucy had taken it. She didn't want to believe that all during their heart-to-heart talk Lucy had sat there, asking for advice, knowing she had stolen something from Patricia. Maybe, thought Patricia, she had just knocked it out of the box earlier that morning.

Patricia checked the floor around her dresser. The necklace was not on the carpet.

Okay, she thought, maybe she knocked it on the carpet and Sammie dragged it off somewhere.

Patricia checked her watch. She didn't have time to tear the place apart looking for it—or to ask Lucy about it. She'd have to deal with it later.

Patricia put on a pair of small silver loop earrings, ran the brush through her thick black curls, then went out to the living room. She grabbed her briefcase and headed out the door, ignoring Lucy's call of good-bye.

Chapter 11

Patricia sat in her truck across the street from Kauffman's Real Estate and Auctioneering Agency, wondering if Elsa was going to show up. The agency was dark, just like all the other buildings on the street. Amber light from a street lamp seeped into her truck, making the lime green of her nephew's toy phone look like an odd shade of brown neon.

Patricia looked at the toy phone and wished for a second that the phone really worked. She'd call up her nephew and make silly kissy-huggy noises in the phone at him, and reassure her brother and sister-in-law that she really would visit them before the summer was over. And she'd mean it this time.

Patricia took a deep breath, trying to clear her mind. Normally the quietness of watching a dark street for movement didn't make her this restless, this lonely. Maybe the feeling came from the conversation with Lucy before she left, knowing what Lucy was going through and knowing she couldn't really help.

Or maybe, she thought, her jumpiness came from a tightness in her gut, and the feeling that something was wrong with this case. She kept waiting for something to happen, hoping that if she just looked at the facts right, she could know what it would be, and prevent it. But all she really knew so far was that whoever had purchased the hatpins had used a name that had also been used to rent the room where Andy Lawson had been murdered. She couldn't be sure the person who bought the hatpins was the one sending the notes. She couldn't be sure that Andy had really rented the motel room; perhaps someone besides Andy had rented the room and met Andy there. The only thing she could be sure of was that something connected the hatpins, the motel room, Andy, and Friedrich.

She flicked on the overhead light, glanced at the clock on her dash and at her watch, then flicked the light off. Eight-thirty or 8:32, depending upon which timepiece she wanted to trust.

Five minutes later she saw a figure, its identity lost in the darkness, moving toward the front door of the Kauffman Agency. She couldn't tell if the person was male or female. At the door the figure paused, then it opened, and the figure slipped in. In the dim light Patricia wasn't sure if the person had opened the door with a key, or if he or she had been let in.

Patricia got out of her truck. Once outside of the truck, she paused, considering where the figure might have come from. She hadn't heard any traffic except for the distant hum of cars on the cross street. Whoever it was had walked. Someone was being careful not to be seen coming to the agency. Elsa?

She crossed the street. The door to the agency was slightly ajar; whoever had let themselves in, or been let in, hadn't shut the door. Haste or carelessness? She knocked lightly on the door, waited. Nothing happened. She stepped inside.

Voices, male and female, came from upstairs, where Elsa and Friedrich's offices were located. A light was on in the back. Elsa's office was at the back of the house, too; that must be where the man and woman were meeting. She wouldn't have been able to see the light from the street.

She moved back to the door, putting one foot outside, just in case she was interrupting a meeting the participants would feel compelled to make her run from. "Hello?" she called. The voices quieted immediately.

"Hello? I came here to meet Elsa."

The upstairs floors creaked beneath footsteps, and a figure appeared at the top of the stairs. A light came on suddenly, flooding the stairwell, the entryway, and Patricia's eyes with bright light. Patricia squeezed her eyes shut, a reflex in the sudden light. When she opened them and blinked a few times, she saw Brenda at the top of the stairs, smiling slightly as if amused by the fact that she had left Patricia, for a moment, both blind and vulnerable.

"Elsa," Brenda said, "isn't here."

"She was supposed to meet me here forty-five minutes ago."

"There must be some mistake." Brenda's words slurred together, and she swayed dangerously for a second. She grabbed the top of the banister. Brenda had been drinking.

Patricia moved from the door and up one step. She was determined to find out who was with Brenda. "No mistake. Elsa set the time and place herself."

Brenda didn't react, just blinked a couple times, and stood unsteadily at the top of the stairs.

"You know, I'm actually quite worried about her," Patricia said. "Elsa seems so reliable." She moved up two more steps. "Maybe we should call her at home and see if she's okay."

"No! Don't come up!"

"I'll just take a minute to call her, Brenda. Aren't you worried about your sister?"

Brenda half laughed, half snorted at that. "Dear little Elsa? Daddy's best girl? She can take care of herself. Don't let her weak image fool you. She's tougher than you think."

That temporarily stopped Patricia. At the auction Brenda had called Elsa weak. Now there was an undertone of bitter jealousy, and a different image of Elsa being given. Patricia wondered which image Brenda really believed. She took another step up the stairs.

"Look, I came here to meet Elsa, and I think I ought to find out why she stood me up. I'm coming up there to use the phone."

"No—"

The floorboards creaked again, and Tom Nielson appeared at the top of the stairs.

"What is going on here? Didn't Brenda ask you to leave?"

Brenda looked around at Tom, opened her mouth to say something, then clamped it shut suddenly. She looked down at Patricia, her expression suddenly tired and resigned to whatever else the night would bring.

"Oh, never mind. Come on up." Brenda turned and went back down the hall. Tom, looking confused, followed her. Patricia went up the stairs. Brenda hadn't wanted her to know Tom was there. Were they meeting to carry on their affair? Or for something more? Patricia went back to Elsa's office.

Tom was in the visitors' chair, Brenda behind the desk. Papers were strewn across the desk in disarray.

"As you can see, we were working. Special project," Brenda said. She was holding a pen and tapping it against the desk.

"In Elsa's office? Don't you have your own?"

"Yes, but most of the important papers are kept here. I know where everything is in this office," Brenda said, smiling smugly. "Elsa and Daddy don't know I know that. Isn't that funny?"

"Brenda, I don't think you should—" Tom started.

"Shut up! I'll say what I want!" Brenda frowned at Tom, then looked back at Patricia and smiled sweetly. "Poor Tom. He's broke. He needs our money to do the development, and I think it bothers him. I think it does. But we need his expertise. His brains."

Brenda threw back her head and laughed loudly. Tom clenched his jaw tightly. The man was willing to put up with a lot to get at that money, Patricia thought.

"Patricia probably already knows that," Tom said. "I imagine Friedrich's told her all about it. God knows the man has no respect—"

"Shut up!" Brenda snapped, frowning again. "You were bankrupt when you came here, and you'd be lost without us. I won't hear you put Daddy down."

"Yes, dear," Tom muttered under his breath.

Brenda looked at Patricia and smiled again. "We're working on a special project. Top secret. Make us both rich, eh, Tom? But Tom was late. Awfully late getting here."

"I told you, I had to wait for Anne—"

"Anne's his wife," Brenda said to Patricia. She laughed shortly.

"Look, I'd love to hear more, but I really am getting worried about Elsa," Patricia said. "When's the last time you saw her?"

"End of business, when she and Daddy left together." Brenda frowned, unhappy that her audience did not appear to be interested in the little drama she was determined to act out with Tom.

"And she hasn't been here since?"

"No, I told you. She and Daddy left at five-thirty, just before me. We didn't have any clients scheduled for after that." Brenda frowned. "Why are you asking all these questions anyway? You were fired. You shouldn't even be here."

It took a few seconds for Brenda's words to register, and when they did, the shock Patricia felt showed on her face. Brenda laughed.

"Ah, I see. Elsa hasn't told you yet."

"I don't understand—"

"Daddy told me this morning that he'd asked Elsa to fire you." Brenda shook her head and clicked her tongue. "You see, you made one big mistake. You suggested that maybe Andy wasn't such a nice guy. Maybe we're not such a big happy family. And that's one suggestion Daddy can't take."

"Brenda—you shouldn't have said anything. You've had too much to drink," Tom said.

"I got thirsty waiting for you—okay, darling?" Brenda looked at Patricia and said, "You know, you look really shocked. I wouldn't have thought anything could throw you. Elsa didn't tell you!"

Brenda's laughter was crackling and hard, and quickly turned into a fit of coughing, a smoker's hacking cough. When she finally got past the coughing jag, she looked up at Patricia again, her eyes watering. "That's great, just great. Elsa was holding out on Daddy, not following his orders! Wait until he finds out."

Patricia took a deep breath. She was angry, angry at Elsa

for not telling her immediately, for not meeting her here like she had said, and at Brenda and Tom and Friedrich and the whole crazy bunch. But she kept her voice under control. "Tell Elsa I'll send my final bill tomorrow."

"Oh, yes, I will," said Brenda. She started laughing and coughing again.

Patricia turned to leave, determined to get out of the Kauffman office as quickly as possible and go to Dean's for iced coffee and some comfort. She had never been fired from a case before.

But as she left Elsa's office she noticed something that made her pause. Friedrich's office door was ajar, and the light was on.

Patricia frowned. Had Elsa been in there this whole time listening to the conversation? She was not going to be made to look like a fool!

She went up to the door and opened it without knocking, started in, then stopped abruptly.

Friedrich, his crippled leg twisted at an odd angle beneath him, was sprawled in front of his desk. He was wearing a brown polyester suit, dressed for his work, implying that he'd never left the office as Brenda had said.

She approached the body carefully, slowly, knowing already that he was dead. Fighting back the sickness that rose to her throat, Patricia knelt down by Friedrich's body. There was a gash at the top of his head, the hair matted with blood.

Friedrich had been stabbed repeatedly in the throat and chest. Sticking out of his chest was a hatpin. Patricia wondered if he had hit his head while falling after being stabbed, or had been hit over the head and then stabbed.

And then Patricia drew back, finally seeing that the hatpin's design was an angel head with a mawkish grin, a twin to the first hatpin that had come with its threatening note for Friedrich.

Chapter 12

Except for the photocopy machine where the stove used to be, most of the kitchen at the Kauffman Real Estate and Auction Agency had been left intact. The room was narrow, with old green-and-white tile and worn white curtains, but it was a pleasant enough break area, offering refrigerator, microwave, coffeepot.

Patricia sat at the kitchen table, waiting to be called to talk to Detective John Derrick again. She had been directed to wait in the kitchen after her initial interview with him. An officer stood on just the other side of the door, in the agents' work area, where Derrick was interviewing Brenda and another detective was interviewing Tom. Other police officers were carefully going over the murder scene upstairs as well as the rest of the building.

Patricia had given Derrick the bare facts about who she was, how she had found Friedrich, what she was doing there. He had not seemed pleased to learn that she was a private investigator.

It was too close and hot in the kitchen. Patricia went to the backdoor, opened it, and stepped outside, leaving it ajar so she could hear Derrick come for her.

Patricia sat down on the patio and took a deep breath. The air, thick with heat and humidity, was heavily perfumed with roses. In the light from the kitchen she could make out a rosebush. She got up, went over and looked at the rosebush, and realized why the scent had been so strong. The bush had been trampled, several of its branches and blooms crushed into the ground, along with the annual flowers planted around it.

Her first thought was that Elsa would be upset when she saw her little garden crushed. Patricia had no reason to assume the garden was Elsa's, except she was the only one at the agency likely to spend time on a garden. Patricia smiled ruefully. So she and Elsa did have something in common besides the hatpins. They both kept small flower gardens.

Her next thought was to wonder who had trampled the garden. Could be someone from the agency, stepping out back for a smoke, careless. Or the murderer, escaping out the backdoor, upon hearing Brenda enter the house? There were no signs of forced entry at the backdoor, and Patricia couldn't recall any at the front door. Whoever killed Friedrich must have had easy access to the building. That implied a key, someone who worked here, someone who knew Friedrich intimately.

Brenda and Tom, Patricia thought immediately. It seemed odd that Brenda hadn't noticed the light in her father's office before, gone in to investigate, or at least to turn off the light, then noticed the body. Had she really been that distracted by Tom's being late to meet her?

Or, thought Patricia, Tom could have killed Friedrich, then left to clean up and come back. That could explain his lateness as much as his wife needing him.

Either one of them, together or alone, could have gotten in a fight with Friedrich, perhaps about money, perhaps about his control over Tom. Brenda defending her lover, finally angry enough to strike back at her father, maybe thinking she would inherit some or all of the agency . . . or Tom, finally snapping under Friedrich's rule . . . but why kill him with a hatpin? The scenario had possibilities in light of Friedrich's death alone, but not when taken in consideration with the hatpins. And it didn't make sense that either of them would kill Friedrich, then let Patricia upstairs so easily.

The whole situation was making less and less sense. How was Andy, and possibly the $100,000, connected to the hatpins and Friedrich's murder? Friedrich's death made the hat-

pins even more mysterious. Were they a ruse, simply meant
to create confusion while the killer carefully planned a murder for cold, calculated reasons?

Or had the hatpins and the messages really been meant to
frighten Friedrich? That implied revenge of some sort, with
the hatpins as a symbol for why the revenge was necessary,
just as the trampled garden implied that the killer had needed
to leave in a hurry.

Either way Friedrich's murder had been premeditated, and
connected in some way to the hatpins. Patricia wondered if
the killer had left the angel's-head hatpin sticking in Friedrich's chest only because he or she had to leave quickly, or
if that had been the final hatpin message.

Lieutenant Detective John Derrick was a handsome man,
who did his best to obscure the fact behind a scowl, a grimly
set mouth, thick black-rimmed glasses. He sat at an agent's
desk, sifting through some notes, pointedly ignoring Patricia.

She stirred restlessly, clearing her throat. John looked up
at her over his glasses.

"Pardon the delay. I was just looking over some notes
from another case."

"There's one more pressing right now than this one?"

"It's a case related to this one, at least because of the
association with the agency. Andy Lawson. I understand from
Brenda that you were hired to investigate his disappearance
for the Kauffmans."

"Yes. And the disappearance of a hundred thousand dollars from the agency's safe. Turning up missing at the same
time Andy did."

John frowned. "Brenda didn't mention the hundred thousand."

"No? Well, that's what I was after—Andy and the money.
Friedrich presumed Andy took the money and disappeared.
I wasn't so sure, especially after he turned up dead and ba-
sically cashless. But then I believe it became your case."

John raised his eyebrows, so they just topped his glasses.

"Not mine. It's out of my jurisdiction. But because Andy worked and lived here, we cooperated in the investigation with the Miller's Crossing police. Your name came up the other day, though. You were at the Blue Bird Motel in Miller's Crossing asking questions about Andy's murder. Seems one of the investigators learned that upon paying another visit to the motel."

Patricia frowned. "What does my visit have to do with tonight?"

John tossed his pen back down on the desk, leaned back in his chair, and crossed his arms. "I was hoping you could tell me," he said.

"I went down there because the Kauffmans—actually Elsa Kauffman—hired me for more than finding Andy. Her father had been getting poison-pen notes stuck on hatpins."

John lurched forward in his chair suddenly, leaning his weight on his crossed arms. "Hatpins?"

"Yes. Like the one used to stab Friedrich. In fact, one was its exact twin."

John leaned back in his chair again, but didn't relax. "Poison-pen notes on hatpins."

"Yes. Elsa had been shielding her father from getting them, because she knew they would upset him."

"So she brought them to you, for you to find out who was sending them."

"Yes."

"And not to the police."

"She was afraid for authorities to get involved—she thought you'd either laugh her off, or insist on talking with her father. And she didn't want that."

Patricia rubbed the white diagonal scar on her chin. "If you didn't know the Kauffmans, it's hard to explain. Image is very important to them, especially Friedrich. The thought of anyone criticizing him or his family—of suggesting there might be a problem—was enough to set him off."

"I see," said John slowly. He clicked his pen. "So these hatpin notes—were they threatening?"

"Vaguely. The hatpins had been in the family. They were

Friedrich's mother's until they were sold at auction last summer. Elsa knew who had bought them—an antique dealer.''
Patricia settled back in her chair. "I paid him a visit and fortunately he knew who had bought them. A man named Jack Grierson.''

"Same name Andy used to register at the Blue Bird Motel.''

Patricia nodded. "I wanted to find out what I could about whoever was posing as Jack Grierson. Assuming it wasn't Andy. And I don't think it was.''

John stopped clicking his pen. "Someone other than Andy using a phony name? Why would you think that?''

Patricia smiled. "The name's not phony. Belongs to a real person, who has been dead a long time. Killed in Vietnam. And I think it was someone else besides Andy who used the name. For one thing, sending vaguely threatening notes doesn't fit Andy's history. He'd go for direct bribery or extortion or thievery. And hanging around in a motel for two weeks doesn't fit him either. He'd have taken the money and run. Maybe he was working with someone, maybe he accidently crossed paths with the killer. I don't know. I do think the answer to his and Friedrich's death lies in figuring out who would use the name Jack Grierson as a cover. And what the hatpins mean. It's like a symbol of some sort.''

"You are thorough. And perceptive.''

"Thank you.''

"You are also treading a little too closely to police turf.''

"Was. I'm off the case.''

John frowned. "I don't get it.''

"I can't claim a sudden case of a need to do the right thing and turn it all over to you guys.'' Patricia smiled ruefully. "I was fired from the case.''

John shook his head. "This is getting confusing. You were fired. Then why were you here tonight?''

"I didn't know I was fired until I got here. I had an eight o'clock meeting with Elsa. Brenda and Tom told me.''

"Seems everyone knew but you.''

"Seems so." Patricia folded her arms, irritated at the smile that had flickered briefly across the detective's face.

John clicked his pen a few more times, then tossed it down on the desk.

"Elsa Kauffman never showed up to meet you?"

"No."

"Or called to say she'd be late?"

"No."

"Did you try to get ahold of her?"

Patricia frowned. "Never got the chance."

"I see." John looked up at the ceiling, as if studying it. Then he looked back at Patricia suddenly and sat forward, leaning across the table toward her. "Did it ever occur to you that Elsa herself might have created the notes, brought them to you?"

Patricia pressed her fingers to her temples. Elsa could have brought her notes like that, to imply an outside threat, to have someone else believe there was such a threat. Then, perhaps out of anger and hatred over so many years spent under Friedrich's jurisdiction, spent catering to his demands, she could have murdered her father. And Patricia would be the unwitting character witness, the one willing to defend her as incapable of committing such an act.

Patricia swallowed hard, twice. Not Elsa. It was too hard to believe. But dammit, where was she? Had she committed the murder, then, appalled at her act, disappeared somewhere without bothering to create a decent alibi?

"Are you all right, Ms. Delaney?"

Patricia looked up at John, forced herself to focus on him. "Fine. It's just a bit—hot in here."

"Yes. I suppose it is. That's all, Ms. Delaney. Except I want you down at the police station as soon as possible tomorrow morning, with the hatpins and everything else you've got." He looked back down at his notes. She was dismissed.

Patricia stood and headed for the door, forcing herself to keep a normal pace. She wanted to get the hell out of there as quickly as possible. She wanted to run, and forget she had ever met the Kauffmans.

Chapter 13

Lucy was still up when Patricia got home, sitting in the family room.

"You're not tired?" Patricia asked, crossing to the desk and tossing her briefcase on it. She had hoped she could postpone asking Lucy about the necklace until the next morning; after the night's events she wasn't prepared for a possible confrontation with her niece.

"I was waiting up for you."

"You didn't have to do that, although it's nice. I have to say this was one hell of a night—"

Patricia turned and stopped in midsentence when she saw Lucy's expression. Whatever had compelled Lucy to wait up for her was not positive. Anger had tightened her face into a cold, hard mask. She had been like that for a while, Patricia realized, and then she saw the letters. They were strewn about Lucy on the couch in complete disarray.

Patricia settled slowly into the white wicker rocker. "Oh," she said simply.

"I found these," Lucy said, gesturing over the lot of the letters.

"You couldn't just find them. They were in a box in the closet in the room you're using."

Lucy nodded. "Yes. I was looking for the guitar you said was in the closet. Thought it might be nice to play around with a guitar tonight, not much else to do, you know? I found the guitar, but I knocked over the box containing these." She gestured at the letters like they were so much disgusting litter.

Patricia sighed, closed her eyes, and leaned back in the rocker. Most of the letters were from her siblings, parents, friends, harmless little *how are you's*? and *sorry it's been so long* missives dating from the present back to her high-school days. She'd just thrown them in a box in the closet all these years, meaning to sort through them someday. Lucy wouldn't give a damn about those letters. The letters from Maureen, from seventeen years ago, from before Lucy's birth, those letters were what had intrigued her, kept her reading, looking for more scraps of the hurtful truth.

Some truths were better left uncovered. It was advice Patricia might give to a few of her clients if she didn't have a code of never passing judgment on a client's need to know. But the truth always lured, even when ultimately it might do more harm than good.

To Lucy the truth, from the letters, would seem clear enough. Maureen had not wanted her. At seventeen, Maureen had eloped with a young man to a different state, where they didn't need parental consent at the time to marry. Soon after Lucy was born, the marriage went sour, and Maureen found herself scared, broke, and abused. She'd contacted Patricia, trusting her when she felt she could trust no one. She wanted to give the baby up. Patricia, fifteen years old at the time, had told her parents about Maureen's troubles, not sure what else to do. Her parents convinced Maureen to keep the baby, which she did, and stayed in the marriage, until her husband finally took off. Maureen had written Patricia, berating her for a betrayal of trust, saying her life would be better without Lucy. Since then, Patricia had been tied to Maureen by more than sisterly love; she had kept a sense of guilt and responsibility for the mess Maureen's life had remained.

Patricia opened her eyes and looked at Lucy, who was still staring at her with the same cold, impenetrable mask. "You shouldn't have read them. In fact, you shouldn't have been looking through my stuff. That box of letters was securely stashed on the closet shelf."

"What are you accusing me of?" Lucy's laugh was forced

and bitter. "After what I found, how could you—you don't really care about me—no one does—" Suddenly the mask crumbled, tears were streaming down her face.

Patricia rubbed her fingers across her temples. Her head was starting to hurt. She wished for a glass of iced coffee, strong on the bourbon, like only Dean could make it. She wished she had never agreed to let Maureen send Lucy here. She wished she had never heard of the Kauffman family. She wished her life was calm and peaceful, like it had been before either the Kauffmans or Lucy had entered it.

One problem at a time, she told herself. Lucy was here, sobbing now, and wishing her away wasn't going to help either Lucy or Maureen or herself.

"My mother didn't want me! She wanted to get rid of me! I wasn't meant to be born! She and I would both have been better off if I hadn't been born. She—she's said that before when she was angry. . . ." Lucy's sobbing dissolved into blubbering.

Patricia went to the kitchen and poured two glasses of iced decaffeinated coffee, no bourbon. It wouldn't be as good as Dean's, but it would have to do. She went back out to the family room and held one of the glasses out to Lucy.

"Here, drink some of this."

"I don't want it . . . I don't want anything. . . ."

"Oh, buck up, and take it, dammit! And if you want me to talk with you about this, calm down!"

Lucy looked stunned, but took the glass and quieted down. Patricia settled back in the rocker, took a long drink, then pressed the glass against her head. Its coolness soothed away some of the throbbing in her temples.

"All right, Lucy, here's the bottom line. When I said no pity parties after I picked you up at the bus station, I meant it."

Lucy just looked at her in stony silence, her black eye makeup smeared and her eyes red from crying.

Patricia sighed. "Look, maybe Maureen would have been better off without you, I can't know. Neither can she, neither can you. But you're here. She made the choice to keep you, granted with a little pressure from her family. Maureen has always found a way to be in trouble, to need to be rescued. She'd be that way with or without you. Nobody would accuse Maureen of being a model mother, but she's the one you're stuck with.''

Patricia took another long drink of the iced coffee, studying Lucy while she did so. Lucy still looked at her, her lips pressed together tightly. It was an expression reminiscent of Maureen. Patricia wasn't sure if she was getting through to the kid or not, but she wanted to try. She remembered, sadly, the carefree, happy child Lucy had been.

''As to whether or not you were meant to be born, I don't know that either,'' Patricia said. ''I don't believe in fate. I just believe you do the best you can. You're here, on this earth, maybe in a tougher situation than some kids, but not in the worst situation possible. Maybe your counselor's right, maybe you've gotten in trouble to get attention. You have a choice. You can keep doing that, mess up your life in the process, trying for sympathy. Or you can just get on with it, make the best of your life, like the rest of us.''

''Is that what you do, Auntie Patricia, make the best of it?'' Lucy said it like she was spitting at her.

''Yeah, I guess so.'' Patricia sighed and rubbed her eyes. ''Gather the letters and leave them on the desk. When you want to go to bed, use my room. I'm going to be in the spare room for a while.''

She stood up and headed back to the bathroom.

''Sure, Auntie Patricia.''

Patricia paused on her way to the bathroom. ''And, Lucy, I've discovered a gold necklace of mine is missing. If you see it, I want you to put it back in my jewelry box.''

''Are you saying I took it?''

Patricia looked at Lucy long and hard, until Lucy started to glance away uncomfortably. Lucy began picking up the letters.

''No,'' said Patricia. ''I'm not saying you took it. I'm saying it's missing. I'm going to trust that it will turn up, by the time your visit here is over.'' She waited until Lucy looked up at her again. ''Remember, Lucy, your choice.''

In the bathroom, Patricia stripped slowly, her movements precise and deliberate as she took off each piece of clothing and dropped it in the laundry basket. Then she stepped into the shower. She turned on the cold water only and stood in the icy blast until all heat was driven from her body, until the sense of oppressiveness from the sticky summer night, the Kauffmans' office, the encounter with Lucy and the past was, at least temporarily, driven from her.

When she got out of the shower, she was shivering. She toweled off and walked naked into the spare room. She shut the door, not bothering to turn on the lights. She moved to her drums and sat down, picked up a stick, and felt its slight weight in her hand.

Then she tapped it against a drumhead. Just one tap, then another, evenly spaced, the sparsest and simplest of rhythms. After a time she picked up the other stick and added a second, syncopated beat. She kept on that way, adding rhythms and patterns, slowly building the sound pattern with sticks and drums and cymbal, letting it draw her in bit by bit, letting it slowly obliterate the thoughts and questions in her mind, letting it override the throbbing in her temples, until at last her playing became frenzied and wild, until the coldness left her body and she was warm and sweating again, until finally she lost awareness of her mind, her body, the room, time, anything except the rhythms that came from the deepest core of her being.

Chapter 14

Patricia sat on the edge of the couch, balancing the paper plate on her knees, and realized she didn't really want anything on the plate, not the green bean casserole made with mushroom soup and canned fried onions, not the lime Jell-O salad, not the ham. But she had passed under the watchful eyes of the sadly smiling neighborhood ladies in the Kauffman kitchen, and she knew she was expected to take some of everything. This was, after all, the Midwest.

She had gone to Friedrich Kauffman's funeral because Brenda had called her, saying that Elsa was distraught and asking to talk with her. Friedrich was buried in Spring Grove Cemetery in a plot he'd long ago reserved next to his wife. It was fitting, Patricia had thought during the service, that he had been laid to rest surrounded by descendants of the country he had emigrated from: Schullers and Oberkleins and Bauers and Aufdenkamps were clustered near the Kauffman family plot. Had he picked his burial spot with the idea that in a sense he'd be returning home? Patricia had also noted that a headstone waited for Elsa, her name and birth date already etched into the gray stone, although there were no stones for her brother or her sister. Elsa's parents had assumed that Elsa would not have a husband to be buried by, that she would not have final wishes of her own to be carried out. Patricia wondered how long ago the plots had been purchased.

At the funeral Elsa had remained between Brenda and a man Patricia did not recognize. After the funeral Patricia had

111

started to walk to her truck, when Brenda ran up to her and asked her to come here, to the Kauffman house.

A huge man, sitting in a brown recliner, was discoursing on how he knew Friedrich well, having been his neighbor for years. The recliner, thought Patricia, had probably been Friedrich's, and he would resent seeing the man stuffed into it. She was also certain that the man had not known Friedrich well. She suspected no one had.

She imagined Friedrich in the recliner, comfortably situated with feet up and a drink at his side, watching the television or reading or snoozing. He had sat there, seeing the fireplace with the brass pot of pothos ivy and the bric-a-brac on the mantel, the nubby pink couch, the window with the sheer white curtains, year after year, ordering Elsa to bring him a drink or answer a question. She could see Elsa, sitting timidly on the edge of the pink couch, or working nervously in the cramped kitchen with the green-and-silver-flecked tile and outdated appliances, waiting to respond to whatever her father might request.

Patricia shivered at the image. But this was partially what she had come here for, wasn't it, she told herself. She had wanted to see how the Kauffmans lived, to learn what she could about them from their surroundings. She had sent the final bill to Elsa the day before, but the unanswered questions still nagged at her. Why had Brenda and Tom been meeting at the agency the night of Friedrich's murder—for more than a tryst, surely? They had appeared to be working on something. Why hadn't Elsa shown up at the agency at all?

Being in the Kauffman house made her again curious about something else. Friedrich was successful enough that he could afford a much better house than one in the older section of Blue Ash. He had very much cared about his family's image, yet he had never moved up to a nicer home, as he and his agents would have advised clients to do.

"I thought you were fired. What are you doing in this house?" The high-pitched voice was male, one Patricia did not recognize. She looked up, ready to fire back a retort, but drew in a sharp breath when she saw the man.

The lime Jell-O salad wobbled dangerously on her plate, threatening to topple to the floor.

It was Friedrich, arisen from the grave and returned as an angel, still tall, thin, and pale, with white hair and ice-blue eyes, but standing straight and evenly, his right arm whole again, years of age dropped from his face. Patricia squeezed her eyes shut hard, then reopened them. No, of course it wasn't Friedrich.

She forced a steady smile. "You must be Henry Kauffman." It figured that Friedrich's only son would introduce himself in this way. "My name is—"

"I know who you are. Brenda described you to me. What are you doing here?"

Patricia frowned and put the plate of untouched food on the coffee table in front of her. The large man in the brown recliner and the two older women at the end of the couch were now staring at her in alarm.

She stood up and looked evenly into Henry's expressionless eyes.

"I'm here because Brenda asked me here. She said Elsa was upset—"

"Elsa is distraught and under a doctor's care. She is in no state to see anyone. And it seems, Ms. Delaney, that one of my father's last requests was that you be fired from his service. Given that I am the family lawyer and executor of the estate, I think it is within my rights to request that you stay away from the Kauffman family."

Patricia took a deep breath and snatched her purse off the couch and slung it over her shoulder. "Believe me, Mr. Kauffman, you won't need a restraining order to ensure that."

She started to move past him when another man came in the family room and blocked the doorway.

"Excuse me," she said abruptly.

"Are you Patricia Delaney?"

"Yes. Now, if you'll get out of my way—"

"Just a minute." He looked past her at Henry. "The doctor says Elsa is fine now for visitors."

Henry didn't say anything. Patricia studied the man blocking her way. He was an inch shorter than she, medium build, tan, with curly auburn hair and brown eyes. He was the man who had stayed by Brenda and Elsa at the funeral. And she wouldn't have any problem knocking him out of her way if he didn't move by the time she mentally counted to ten. One, two, three . . .

"C'mon, Henry," he said. "It will do Elsa some good. The doctor gave her a tranquilizer, but I'm sure she'll rest better if she has a chance to talk with Patricia."

Henry still did not respond. Apparently he was deciding what to do. Patricia didn't give a damn which way he chose. Four, five, six . . .

"Fine," Henry said finally. "But not for more than five minutes, and you escort her to Elsa's room, Kurt. And make sure she leaves right after she talks with Elsa."

Henry walked around Patricia, and Kurt jumped out of his way as he strode out of the room. Kurt smiled at Patricia sympathetically. "I'm Kurt Knepper. Want to catch your breath before you talk with Elsa?"

Patricia was silent as she studied the man. So this was Kurt, Andy's deskmate, Friedrich's cousin once-removed, who had been on vacation in Florida for the past few weeks. She would have been interested in talking with him a week ago. Now she was irritated, at herself for coming here, at him for being her rescuer. She would rather have had it out with Henry, even though it wouldn't have done any good.

"I'm not sure I'm going to talk with Elsa," Patricia said finally.

Kurt looked concerned. "Don't take the fact that Henry can act like a prick sometimes out on Elsa. She really wants to talk with you." He flashed a toothy grin at her. "Let's go out on the back porch. You can catch your breath there, decide what you want to do."

Was she being manipulated more by staying or by leaving? It seemed that anyone related to the Kauffman family, even a distant cousin, could make her feel that way. Patricia followed Kurt, fighting back anger.

Out on the tiny back porch, Patricia blinked to adjust to

the brightness of the day. She hadn't realized how dark and close it had been in the small family room.

A cluster of adults stood in the backyard. Two little boys and a girl played on the grass, chasing each other and laughing and calling in some game of their own devising.

Patricia sensed that this was the first life the backyard had seen in a long, long time. There were no flowers, no garden, no bird feeders or baths. No barbecue grill on the back patio, no wind chimes in a tree, no croquet set or badminton net. No lawn furniture for sitting in on a summer's dusky evening to listen to crickets or watch fireflies—nothing that indicated the backyard was ever used for any pleasure, just a perfect tiny slope of weed-free green yard. A dog barked from down the street. It was the sort of sound, thought Patricia, that would have set Friedrich's teeth on edge and sent him back inside to his small, quiet family room where Elsa could tend to his needs.

"Sorry we had to meet in such a—tense situation."

"What? Oh." Patricia looked over at Kurt. "Is there any other kind with the Kauffman family?"

Kurt laughed. "Probably not. But they're not all bad. In fact, they've been very good to me. I—was kind of drifting in Florida. In and out of jobs, not sure what I wanted to do with my life, a few bad affairs. That whole trip. Then I came up here last year for Great-Aunt Gertrude's funeral, started getting to know the Kauffman family again—I'd been away for quite a while—and pretty soon Friedrich offered me a job, mostly working on maintenance on his rental units until I could get my real-estate license—"

"Kurt, I don't mean to be rude, but why are you telling me all of this?" Patricia asked.

He laughed again, looking chagrined. "Sorry. It's just like I said, the Kauffmans have been good to me. After my parents—died—when I was a kid, Friedrich and his wife took me in. I don't remember much about that time—I don't really remember my parents—but I know Elsa was especially sweet to me, like a little sister. Then I moved on to live with other relatives, but I've never forgotten how good they were. Elsa's kind of like a sister to me now. And I'm really worried about her. I thought maybe you could help. . . ."

"I see," Patricia said. She remembered Elsa telling her that Kurt's father had killed his wife, Kurt's mother, then later himself. That had to be a difficult, confusing time for him as a child, and she could see why he'd be grateful to the Kauffmans now, even if his memories of the time were incomplete or vague.

"Why are you so worried about Elsa, besides the fact that she needs a doctor's care right now to calm down?"

"It's these hatpins. . . ." Kurt paused.

"She told you about them?"

"Yes. But she won't talk to the police about them."

"I've told the police everything I know about them."

"Yes. I figured you might have. But she won't talk to them. They scare her. And I'm afraid they think she might have killed her father."

"What do you think?"

"I—I don't know. It's hard to believe, but Elsa has always been so—fragile. This isn't the first time she's needed a doctor's care for emotional distress. And Friedrich did run her life, and treat her pretty harshly at times. Who knows? Maybe she did send the messages and has convinced herself someone else did, then got into some argument with Friedrich—I don't know."

"If you suspect anything, and have any concrete reason to believe at all that Elsa killed her father, you should talk to the police."

"Yes. I'm aware of what I should do—legally. But like I said, Elsa is like a sister to me. I want her to be okay—whatever she might have done. Not that she did, but if she did, it would have been while she was—out of her head, you know?"

Kurt sighed, stared out at the perfect square of lawn. "Look, Elsa trusts you. Admires you, even. She's told me that. I just got the call in Florida a few days ago about Friedrich and got up here yesterday afternoon. I'm staying here temporarily to make sure Elsa will be okay, since Brenda and Henry are too—preoccupied to do so. All she has talked about has been her feeling that she was a disappointment to Friedrich all her life, and about you, how much she looks up to you.''

Kurt turned suddenly, looking beseechingly at Patricia. ''If she's got anything to confess, she'll confess it to you, or it will eat her alive. I just want to ask you to listen to her, see if you can get her to open up.''

Patricia looked out over the slip of yard, trying to concentrate on the children playing on the perfect green grass, on the dog barking somewhere down the street. It was the most normal scene possible from middle-class America, yet as she imagined Elsa in her room on the second floor also looking out at the backyard, the children's voices faded, and the image of them playing suddenly seemed surreal. It was as if a veneer of innocence thinly coated the scene, a coating that could easily be scratched away to reveal something sinister and frightening and complex that might have taken place in this house years ago.

Patricia shook her head, and the children's voices returned. She took a deep breath. ''I'll talk with Elsa. I'll encourage her to cooperate with the police. But if she tells me anything of importance to the case, I'll talk with them myself.''

''I understand,'' Kurt said quietly.

They went back in the house. After the brightness and openness of outside, the house seemed dark and close. Patricia followed Kurt up a narrow stairway to a small landing. Kurt knocked on the first bedroom door to the left.

''Elsa?'' he called.

There was a moment of silence, then a feeble ''come in.''

Kurt opened the door and stood aside. ''I'll be out here if you need me,'' he said.

Patricia went in the room, shut the door, and immediately caught her breath. The room was a stereotypical little girl's fantasy room. The wallpaper was pink, with stripes and roses. The white four-poster bed had a canopy and bedspread that where white and covered with pink roses. Piled on the bed were pillows in various shades of pink and rose, and a few tattered, stuffed animals. A white wicker rocker, also filled with stuffed animals and pillows, sat off to the side. On a dresser was a stack of photo albums. One of the albums lay open. In the arc of light from the lamp on the nightstand was a large medicine bottle. Tranquilizers, Patricia realized.

Elsa stood at the window, still in her high-necked black dress. She stared out over the backyard, at the children playing. Their voices were muted, but audible, up here. A chill, despite the hot stuffiness of the room, danced over Patricia's skin.

"Elsa," she said softly.

Elsa stood perfectly still, not saying anything for a moment. When she spoke, her voice was scratchy. "I'm glad you came to talk with me."

"I'm sorry about your father."

Elsa turned from the window, moved to the edge of the bed, and sat down. She had a slow, sleepy look on her face, a lopsided weak smile, droopy eyes. The tranquilizers were casting their spell. Patricia wondered just how many she had taken.

"My father," Elsa said. "This seems like a dream."

Patricia sat on the edge of the bed next to Elsa. "Give it time."

"I've been looking through my grandmother's old albums and things. Maybe I shouldn't . . . Father wouldn't like it. . . ." Elsa looked around the room suddenly, a cheek muscle twitching, her eyes darting, like an animal suddenly panicked upon realizing it's trapped. "I don't know if I can live here alone. But I've always lived here. Except for a time, in college, then a little after. But that doesn't seem real. It seems like I've always lived here. Now I'll have to sell the house. . . ."

"You don't have to worry about that now," Patricia said. "You've got plenty of time, and Brenda can help you."

"Yes," Elsa said. Her voice sounded distracted, like she was in another world of thought. She looked at Patricia suddenly. "What's the most dangerous thing you've ever done?"

"What?" Patricia said, surprised at the question and the forcefulness with which it was asked.

"The most dangerous thing you've ever done."

Patricia stood up, went over to the window, and looked out. The children were gone. The backyard was as it had been before Friedrich's death, a perfect square of grass, unused. She turned around.

"Most dangerous, physically?"

"Yes. I guess."

Patricia took a deep breath. "I was very close to my sister, Maureen, when I was a kid. She was kind of wild. We both were." She paused. "Have you ever noticed that underneath a highway overpass there are these bars, like supports?"

Elsa looked confused, shook her head.

"Well, they're there. Maureen dared me one day to climb up underneath and cross over the road below by going hand over hand on those bars. Said she'd be right behind me. I scrambled up, grabbed onto the bar, and focused on crossing. Didn't even hear the cars beneath me. Just crossed."

Elsa stared at her, her eyes wide. She was, Patricia realized, holding her breath.

Patricia laughed. "Obviously I made it."

"And Maureen?"

"When I got to the other side and jumped down, I looked back and saw Maureen. She hadn't crossed. She had stayed on the other side and watched me. Later she told me she didn't think I'd do it." Patricia paused a moment. "I've kept a reminder of the incident. When I jumped down, I fell and cut my chin open." Patricia's fingers briefly touched the white diagonal scar.

"You were brave."

"No, stupid. Risking your life just to show how tough you are is stupid. What about you?"

Elsa looked down, began playing with the sash of her dress. "I wanted to tell you—that's why I asked you—but I'm sure you'll think this is really stupid—"

Patricia sat down next to Elsa on the bed. "No, what I did

was stupid. You can tell me if you want. I'm not going to laugh, Elsa.''

"I—I knew this boy, in high school. Kent.'' Elsa smiled dreamily, closed her eyes, and weaved back. Patricia caught her. The tranquilizers would take over soon, and for some reason it was important to Elsa to tell her this. "Go on,'' Patricia urged gently.

Elsa opened her eyes and again focused on the room, and the present. "Kent. He was so nice. We—we skipped school to go to Coney Island. Rode all the rides. Just rode them over and over. Ate cotton candy and popcorn. And then we went down by the river.'' Her voice was dreamy again. Her eyes narrowed to thin slits. "It was dangerous because if my father had found out I was skipping school . . . with a boy . . .'' Elsa sighed. "I was always such a good girl. Anyway, that's where I was the other night.''

Patricia looked at Elsa, startled. "When you were supposed to meet me at the agency?''

"Yes. Not Coney Island, of course. Down by the river, at Yeatman's Cove. I've being going through old things of my grandmother's—pictures, letters, scrapbooks, in the attic. She saved a lot about her husband. She worshiped him. All that romance. Made me think of Kent, and I wanted to go back. I just sat down by the river, listening to the cars sing.''

Elsa paused and smiled thinly. "Have you ever noticed that—the hum the cars make crossing the bridge?''

Patricia nodded. "Yes. It can be very hypnotic.''

"I forgot about our meeting, everything, once I was there. It took me back—to the time with Kent—'' She weaved back again. "I—I don't feel so good.''

"It's the medicine the doctor gave you,'' said Patricia. "Come on, you should get in bed.''

Elsa nodded obediently, stood up, and fell back on the bed. Patricia helped her back up.

With Elsa leaning on her for support, Patricia pulled back the bed covers. She sat Elsa on the edge of the bed, helped her off with her shoes and dress, and then got her in bed, with the pink rose-covered bedspread tucked around her.

Patricia folded up Elsa's dress and put it on the rocker. She knelt down next to Elsa. "You tell the police what you told me. About where you were that night. And anything else you know. They won't hurt you as long as you tell the truth."

Elsa nodded. With just her head above the comforter and her fingertips curled over the top, she looked like a little girl prematurely aged from some long sickness. "Yes. I should." Her speech was thick and slurred now. "But I thought—I thought somehow my father would find out—then I'd be in trouble. It didn't hit me until today that he is gone—he's really gone."

"You don't have to worry about getting in trouble now, as long as you tell the police everything you know. Cooperate with them, Elsa."

"I wanted you to know where I was that night, Patricia. I didn't want you to think I am, I am irresponsible. . . ."

"I don't think you're irresponsible," said Patricia. Just groggy and drained from the emotional day and tranquilizers. "Listen, I'll come by tomorrow night, eight o'clock, to check on you. Okay?" To hell with Henry's warning to stay away.

"That would be . . . great." Elsa's voice faded off, her eyes shut.

Patricia stayed in the room until Elsa's breath came evenly and deeply. Then she left, shutting the door behind her gently.

"She's sleeping," she told Kurt. He was still outside the room, sitting on the top step.

She raced down the stairs, not wanting to talk to Kurt or Brenda or Henry or anyone else in the Kauffman house, pausing only when she stepped outside to blink at the sudden brightness of the day after the dim closeness of the house.

Chapter 15

The next morning Patricia pressed the page-down key on her computer's keyboard, scanning the lines of text. A doctoral dissertation on *The Nesting, Feeding, and Mating Habits of Ptarmigans* was usually not her idea of exciting reading for Tuesday afternoon, or any other time. But just now she was grinning widely.

So far, the credentials of Alliston College professorial candidate Dr. Arnold Hauser had stood up to scrutiny. Then Patricia ran a search in a database of dissertations and other scientific professional papers. The dissertation Hauser said was his existed, all right. It had just been written by an Everest Morrison fifteen years before.

Patricia selected the dissertation to print, leaned back in her chair, and waited. The document would take some time and money to print, but she was sure it would be worth it to the head of biology at Alliston College, who had just sensed a few things as "off" in his interview with young Dr. Hauser. Patricia would double-check her other findings, explore a few other avenues, but the plagiarized work would be enough to ensure Hauser didn't make it into Alliston. Another college might not decide to use the services of an investigator, so Hauser could still find a position elsewhere. Patricia had read once that nearly half of all résumés or job applications are falsified in some manner. It was a statistic that helped keep her employed.

Patricia stood, stretched, rubbed the back of her neck, and went to her back room to refill her glass with iced coffee. It had been a satisfying morning. She had finished her summaries of the Kauffman cases and moved her notes and summaries into a blue folder, even though the cases were, to the police, very much open. To her, though, they were closed.

Then she had talked with two new clients, one a business owner wanting a company checked out before he went into partnership with it, the other a young woman who wanted to have her lover's past checked out before she got too serious about him. After writing up initial notes and setting up files for those clients, Patricia had gone through some bills, then started her computer search on good old Hauser. It was back to business as usual—no murders, no hatpins, no strange families.

When she went back out to her outer office, she saw that she had rejoiced at the return to normality too soon. In the chair in front of her desk, legs primly crossed, fingertips pressed together and held at his lips, sat Henry Kauffman. He was dressed in a suit, complete with vest, and looked as cool as if it were autumn outside, and not a hot, muggy June day.

He put his hands in his lap. "Your door was unlocked."

"It wasn't open."

"I assume I'm here during office hours," Henry said.

"Office hours are for my clients, most of whom make an appointment before coming."

"May I make an appointment for now?" Henry spread his hands to indicate sincerity.

"Depends upon whether or not you wish to discuss the possibility of becoming a client. If you don't, then leave." Patricia sat down at her desk, verified the dissertation had finished printing, and began the procedure to exit from the database.

"I must say, Ms. Delaney, you have a most unusual way of encouraging business."

Patricia did not look up from her computer screen. "I'm not a starving private eye, if that's your idea of an investigator. I don't need your business, or necessarily want it. And given your statements to me yesterday"—Patricia paused as she finished up her work on the computer, then looked directly at Henry—"you are going to have to sell me. You have five minutes."

A thin smile slowly sliced Henry's face. Like his father, Henry was almost colorless; pale skin, white hair, icy blue eyes. But his skin was loose rather than taut, as if his skull had shrunk away from its covering, and the circles around his eyes were a deep purple, like bruises. His face was pitted from ancient ravages of acne. His smile, almost predatory, reminded Patricia of the one on the angel's-head hatpin.

"I see, Ms. Delaney. Well, that is fair. I'll state my cause as convincingly as I can." Henry coughed, and the smile disappeared from his face. "I came, in part, to apologize. It was an emotional day, losing my father. I was, naturally, upset and said things I shouldn't have."

"I didn't see you at the funeral."

"I have been out of town on business for a few weeks. I had a few items of a pressing nature that I had to clear up," Henry said, as if his excuse should be perfectly understandable.

It wasn't, to Patricia, but she reminded herself that she was not in business to judge potential clients. "All right. Apology accepted."

"Good. I'm glad that's taken care of. My second order of business is of a rather—delicate—nature." He paused, studying Patricia, as if judging one final time whether or not he had made the correct choice in coming to her. "When I learned that I am executor of my father's estate, I was surprised. Except for an occasional minor legal matter or two I have never been involved in my father's business. This was the first time I reviewed the contents of my father's will."

"You didn't draw it up?"

"No, Ms. Delaney, I did not."

"That surprises me. Your father, Brenda, Elsa—everyone kept telling me what a close-knit family yours is. Seems to me Friedrich would want to keep something like that in the family, so to speak."

Henry smiled. "My father was very disappointed that his only son did not wish to go into the family real-estate business. He made that clear by rarely coming to me for legal help.''

''Who did he use?''

Henry's smile widened. ''My partner. My father had—inventive ways to make his feelings clear.''

''I see. And what you've learned about his will concerns you?''

''Yes, portions of it. The house was left to Elsa, with the provision that she retain her present position, or similar one, at the agency, with her present salary and regular raises as long as she desires, until she retires. If she quits, however, she is not to be hired back, and the house becomes mine.''

Patricia shuddered. Elsa had a home and a job as long as she stayed for the rest of her life in her father's business. Even from the grave, Friedrich bound her to the house and business, knowing she would be too weak ever to break from them, even after his death.

''The management of the business,'' Henry continued, ''is left to Brenda. I, however, have ultimate financial and legal authority. I can sell the business at any time, or replace Brenda as I see fit.''

''That's strange. Why would your father—''

''He did not trust Brenda's business judgment. She serves her emotions before anything else and has never been able to overcome that particular weakness. And I imagine it was his way of finally getting me in the business.'' Henry paused, spread out his long fingers, and looked at them, then returned his hands to his lap. He looked amused. ''For my efforts I receive a sum of five thousand dollars, to cover my few past legal consultations and my work for him now and in the future. Do you suppose my father didn't realize the rates I charge?''

Patricia supposed Friedrich, going to Henry's partner all those years, knew full well what his work would be worth. She ignored the question. ''Do you doubt the validity of this will?''

''No, oh no. My partner has assured me that my father's

will is solid and was drawn up under the most legitimate of circumstances ten years ago. It has not been changed suddenly within a few weeks before his death, if that is what you were thinking.''

Patricia shrugged. "It may seem like a cliché, but it happens."

''What concerns me is that my father also requested that one hundred thousand dollars be paid, on the first of June each year, to a man named Leroy Hibberd.''

Patricia lifted her hand to rub the diagonal white scar on her chin thoughtfully, then stopped herself. Under Henry's watchful gaze, she did not want to give in to any nervous habits.

"Do you—or your partner—know why?"

"No. My father would not give a reason. Brenda and Elsa tell me he was a consultant of some sort, but they don't know why my father would leave him this payment. Elsa did tell me that Father, every year, sometimes more often, asked her to withdraw between fifty and a hundred thousand dollars cash from the business's account and leave it for him in the safe.''

''Apparently for this Leroy Hibberd.''

''Apparently.''

That would explain the modest home and office, Patricia thought. If for some reason, and the best reason she could think of was blackmail, Friedrich had needed to deliver that much cash to this man, he could not afford to invest his money elsewhere. He could never be sure Leroy would not want more. She recalled the auction, where Leroy had driven the bid for the farmhouse and acreage higher and higher. Punishment because his $100,000 hadn't been delivered, since it had been stolen from the safe, supposedly by Andy? A reminder that he could, and would, break Friedrich if he had to?

Patricia pulled out a notepad and pen, jotted a few notes. Then she looked back up at Henry. "I suppose you want me to find out everything I can about this Leroy Hibberd."

Henry nodded. "As quickly as possible. And I want you to find out what happened to the hundred thousand."

Patricia frowned. "That's part of the Andy Lawson case, which is now under police investigation. I'm not reinvolving myself with that."

"You're assuming he took the money because he and it disappeared at the same time."

Patricia sighed. "No, I'm not. At least I hadn't. When I tried to convince your father, however, that possibly the disappearance of Andy and the money was coincidence, that possibly someone else in the agency took it, he became irate. Instructed me not to check into anyone else's background in the agency."

"My father could be stubborn," Henry said. "I am more reasonable. Given my new responsibilities, I want to make sure I understand everything about the business, including this Leroy Hibberd. Before he gets another payment, I want to know why he's getting them. And I want to ensure that it really was Andy who took the money, not someone else still in the agency. Check out everyone, thoroughly."

"Does that include your sisters?"

"Yes. Especially Brenda, and Tom Nielson."

Patricia arched an eyebrow. "Any particular reason?"

"Let's just say that Brenda, as I mentioned before, can sometimes put her emotions before anything else. And Tom, from the few times I have met him, does not strike me as the most intelligent or trustworthy character. I'm not sure my father was wise to take him as a partner."

On that point Patricia had to agree with Henry.

"Very well. You have made what you want me to do very clear," she said. "Before I decide to take your case on, however . . ." Patricia allowed herself a brief smile at Henry's surprised reaction. Obviously it never occurred to him that she might not want to work with him. ". . . I have one question. Why did you come back to me for this help? You made your feelings clear day before yesterday. Why not another private investigator?"

Henry intertwined his fingers and smiled stiffly. "Very

simple, Ms. Delaney. As you say, we are a close-knit family—with a profitable business to run. You may have disappointed my father, but you have proven yourself to be discreet, and you already know much of what you need to know to get started. I also checked with some colleagues who have used your services, and your reputation and business are well spoken of. I didn't see the point in engaging another private investigator who might not be as competent or discreet.''

"I see," Patricia said. "I'll take your case, provided that I can have complete access to all records of the Kauffman Agency.''

"Very well. Anything you need.''

"All right, then. Let's review my terms and pricing structure.''

"I have that information already from Elsa. Just bill me.''

"You are a new client," Patricia said. "I go over my terms and pricing structure with each new client.''

Henry smiled, almost appreciatively. "Very well.''

Twenty minutes later they were through with the necessary business, and Henry left.

Patricia looked at the closed door and rubbed the scar on her chin. Henry's request was simple enough, no different, really, than many of her other clients' requests. He wanted her to investigate the employees of the agency and an individual who stood to gain significantly from his father's will. Simple enough.

She went to the back room, retrieved the Kauffman files, and got a new red folder, which, back at her desk, she labeled *Kauffman, Henry*.

Her job was to find the truth, or at least verify and find facts. It was something she happened to be very good at and enjoyed. Henry Kauffman was a client like any other, his request a case like any other. Then why, she wondered, was she trembling as she looked at the Kauffman files on her desk?

She closed her eyes, took several deep breaths, forced herself to regain control of herself. Then she opened her eyes and looked at the computer screen on her desk, its cursor blinking on a blank gray screen, waiting for her to give some command. She brought up her word-processing package, to write up her initial notes for the *Kauffman, Henry* file. Her hands shook as she brought them to the keyboard.

"Right, Minerva. This case—just like any other," Patricia muttered out loud.

Then she shook her head to clear it. When she started talking to the little gray box, even using the name of the Greek goddess of knowledge as an endearment, it was time to get out for some human company. She checked the time on the computer. Ten o'clock. Too early for lunch, but maybe Dean would like some company as he opened up the tavern. She was surprised to realize how much she suddenly wanted his company. But there was so much work to do. . . .

To hell with it. Patricia shut down the computer, which made a sighing sound as the power drained from it. She knew just how it felt. She left the files out on her desk, grabbed her purse, and headed out the door for Dean's Tavern. She'd take an hour or so to clear her head, then plunge back into the Kauffman case.

Chapter 16

The musty smell infused the pink bedroom created long ago for her and Brenda, a room meant to be perfect for perfect little girls, a room never meant to smell of anything more potent than gardenias and carnations from a dance corsage. The smell, which came from the boxes of photographs and scrapbooks and letters Elsa had carted down from the attic, seemed irreverent in the pink room, because it signified the passage of time, and decay. Elsa took a deep breath of the mustiness and smiled.

It was the night after her father's burial, and she was alone. She was finally, really, completely alone. Kurt, her only company since her father's death, had gone back to his apartment the previous night, after everyone else left.

Her mother had died years before, finally succumbing to one of her undiagnosable illnesses. Her grandmother Gertrude had died the year before. Brenda and Henry had both long ago left home.

And at last, Elsa thought, fingering a thin sheet of a yellowed letter, her father had died, too. Somehow she had not fully understood that the others had gone from her life until her father was gone, too. It was only in her mind that she had bound them together, with her in the middle of their circle, not sure where to turn next to help and serve, where the need might be greatest, where the rebuke might be strongest if she failed to please. Her father had been the last link in the imaginary circle, and with him gone, she was released and free.

Tonight was the first night she had fully understood her

freedom. Until now she had been too shocked, too guilty for all the ill thoughts she had had about him, to even think. And the first thing she had chosen to do with her freedom was to bring down to her room the papers and photos she had been furtively reviewing in the attic. It had not yet occurred to her that she was free to take the items from the box into any room in the house, any room at all.

Elsa pressed her fingertips to her temples. She had taken several tranquilizers—two? three? She couldn't really remember—a few hours before, and now she felt light-headed. Maybe she just needed another one. She took one of the pills, washing it down with water from the glass she kept on her nightstand.

She touched the stack of letters. Most of them she had already read in the attic. The letters were yellowed and dry, crumbling at the edges. They were letters her grandmother Gertrude and her husband had exchanged, mostly while he had been away during World War I. She had never known her grandfather, but Grandmother Gertrude had told her much about him. He had been brave, honest, smart. Strong, tall, able-bodied. Tough, but kind and romantic.

Elsa herself had never known romance like that, except vicariously through the romance books she read. The closest she had come had been that day at Coney Island with Kent that she had told Patricia about. Elsa smiled to herself. She hadn't told Patricia the whole story. Part of it she had kept to herself, as she always had. That night she and Kent made love in his parents' house, because his parents were away. It was her first, and only, time. It didn't matter now that she could not remember his last name, just as it hadn't mattered then that only a few weeks later he abandoned her for another, prettier girl who was new to the school. She had, to some degree, experienced the romance she had heard her grandmother describe, over and over.

As a sudden wave of guilt coursed through her, Elsa took a deep breath and willed it to pass. Her father would not like it, that she had these items to look through and cherish. He had gone to his grave thinking that every bit of his parents' past had been destroyed.

She picked up an old photo album, took it with her to the rocking chair, sat down, and began looking through the photos.

At first they confused her. Her grandmother was in the pictures, but as an older woman. Elsa had expected pictures from her grandmother's youth, with her husband, and Friedrich as a baby and young boy. Perhaps in the other albums . . . but then Elsa realized these pictures were of her family. Her father and mother, herself, Brenda, and Henry—a young family, gathered at Christmas, at Thanksgiving, all smiling perfect, posed smiles.

And then Elsa understood. When her father had asked her to destroy the boxes of things that had been her grandmother's, he'd added the photo albums to the boxes, the memorabilia of their family. He'd never thought she would look through the boxes or disobey him.

Elsa closed her eyes, trying to think. Her mother had stopped taking so many pictures as she got older, as if her energy for that, as for everything else, was sucked up by her perpetual, unnamed illnesses. Her father never took pictures. She doubted there was even a camera around the house anymore. Since they never got out old photo albums to review, she would never have missed them.

Her father had wanted her to destroy the photos, perhaps other memorabilia, of his family's past. An entire past, coolly destroyed.

And then the thought scampered across her mind, unbidden, uninvited, but persistent. Why? Why did he want that?

Elsa looked through the photo album, page by page, barely breathing, terrified at what she might see, terrified at how absolutely normal and simple the photos were. There was something horrifying about the family in Easter dress, the family gathered at the beach, celebrating when Henry won the spelling bee, celebrating Brenda's first ballet recital; horrifying, because Elsa knew, with growing dread, that behind the simple normality must lie something that explained why her father wanted all these things to be destroyed.

Elsa turned back to the beginning of the album and began looking through again. And then on page three she saw the photo that made her understand.

Suddenly other memories came back, along with horror at understanding why her father had been murdered, why, in fact, it had been his fate to die as he did. She was, Elsa realized, not the only one who finally remembered, who went back mentally in time to piece together the past and grasp the truth.

Elsa jumped up, dropping the album to the floor, and ran to the bathroom. She threw up, retching into the toilet until she had the dry heaves. When she finally stopped and was steady enough to hold a glass, she rinsed her mouth with water. Then she stared at her pale image in the mirror. She was suddenly scared of being alone.

She straightened up, forced herself to breathe evenly, forced herself to think. She was alone. She had to decide for herself. She had to be calm. She went back to her bedroom and took three more tranquilizers.

And then Elsa smiled to herself. She thought about the last time she had seen Patricia, and their conversation about the most dangerous things they had done. She could top skipping school with a young boy years ago. She could be strong, and brave like Patricia. Elsa went downstairs to the phone.

Chapter 17

Patricia listened to *La Traviata* with her eyes closed, the images of the closing scene playing out as clearly and vividly in her mind as if she were watching the heroine sing her last aria on a stage before her. When the music ended, Patricia remained as she was, curled up in the rocker in her family room. In the silence, the images brought forth by the music slowly faded, until at last she was fully aware of the sounds in the room around her—her breathing, the hum of the refrigerator in the kitchenette, Sammie snoring as he napped at her feet.

After a brief break with Dean, Patricia had spent the rest of the day researching the Kauffman agents, and especially Brenda and Tom, for Henry. Starting with the employee files, she had done the most rudimentary of research on each agent and had turned up little of interest except an unreported misdemeanor here, a dismissal there, but nothing that matched Andy's record of trouble or that suggested a need to take $100,000 from the company safe.

Tom and Brenda were another story. Tom, she learned, had inherited his father's construction and development business, a small but national publicly held company simply called Nielson Homes, Inc. Public records and filings, which Patricia tapped into through databases through her computer, showed that after Tom took over as CEO and president, the company's profits steadily declined.

In another database of newspaper and magazine articles, Patricia found several stories of homeowners suing Nielson Homes when, after spending more than $260,000 for a "quality, custom home," their decks collapsed or electrical wiring shorted out and caused minor fires and damages because work had not been up to building code. In short, Tom had taken a viable company that had the potential to eventually compete with the biggest national construction companies and ran it into the ground, finally bankrupting it and declaring personal bankruptcy as well.

Once she learned that, Patricia asked herself what a man like Tom—not overly bright but proud and somewhat arrogant—might do. One option would be to spend the rest of his days getting by in one job or another, complaining about what "they" had done to him rather than admitting his mistakes. Another would be to latch onto someone, using his charisma to convince that person to help him build his reputation and power again, since he certainly couldn't do it alone, not with his track record.

And that person, Patricia knew, was Brenda Gatts. Tom would want to rebuild his life in the only industry he knew—home construction and development. He had been doing that, to some degree with Friedrich, but he had been impatient with Friedrich's ways.

Patricia started checking real estate records through a realestate database on her computer. She checked Cincinnati and turned up nothing, which didn't really surprise her. Brenda and Tom would not want to risk Friedrich learning of their moonlighting projects. Then she started checking the nearest major city, Columbus. Sure enough, a few minutes of searching turned up thirty-six acres purchased about four weeks before by one Brenda Gatts on the suburban outskirts of Columbus. Brenda could not have afforded the property on her own. One hundred thousand would not have been enough to buy the whole amount, but it certainly would have been enough as a down payment, and Brenda could have secured a loan for a sizable amount if she had forged her father's signature as a cosigner.

What she had learned didn't constitute proof that Brenda and Tom had taken the money, but it would certainly in-

terest Henry. Tomorrow she would start researching Leroy
Hibberd before she paid him a visit.

But tonight Patricia didn't have any obligations, any demands on her time. Lucy had gone into town with Lina Carswell, Patricia's resident landlady and friend, to do some
shopping and then catch a movie. It was just as well that
Lucy had more or less attached herself to Lina; the cold war
continued between them and Lucy could use a mother figure
now, something Patricia was not prepared to offer to be. So
Patricia had the whole evening, alone, to herself. She smiled.
She might just listen to the entire opera again.

She went out to the kitchen and poured herself iced coffee,
minus the bourbon, and then noticed the time on the kitchen
clock: 7:30. She had promised Elsa she'd check on her tonight at 8. Patricia sighed, put the glass of coffee back in the
refrigerator, gathered her keys and purse. She thought about
leaving a note for Lucy and decided against it. Then she left
for the Kauffmans'.

Patricia sat in her Chevy S-10 and looked at the Kauffman
house. It was completely dark, as if no one were home, and
the street was quiet. No one was in sight. Yet she had the
feeling of a presence, of being watched. Perhaps Elsa was
upstairs in her absurdly decorated little girl's room, watching
for her. She sensed Elsa's need to talk with her, much as she
had felt it on the day of Friedrich's funeral. Patricia rubbed
her hands over her bare arms, feeling a sudden chill despite
the warm evening. A T-shirt, she thought ruefully, was usually sufficient clothing in summer. She realized she was letting herself get spooked and stopped rubbing her arms.

On the drive up to Blue Ash, Patricia had continued to try
to sort out Friedrich's murder. Who would want to kill him?
Brenda and Tom came to mind—maybe Brenda had thought
she would inherit the agency, maybe Tom thought with
Friedrich out of the way he could manipulate Brenda to do
things his way. It was possible, but unlikely, that Henry had
killed Friedrich, perhaps out of resentment over his treatment over the years. Leroy Hibberd certainly bore investi-

gating; perhaps after his latest $100,000 installment failed to show up, he decided the best thing to do was to kill Friedrich and collect his money each year, assuming he knew that he was named in the will. Maybe Elsa, snapping after years of subservience, as Detective Derrick had insinuated . . .

No. Patricia didn't believe Elsa could have killed her father, and the others didn't fit either, at least based on what she knew so far. Somehow Friedrich's murder was connected with Andy's, and both of those murders were connected to the hatpins, to something significant that the hatpins symbolized.

Patricia took a deep breath, grabbed her purse, and got out of the truck. Friedrich's and Andy's murder were police business. Her only role here was to make sure that Elsa was all right, as she had promised. No use putting it off, no matter how uncomfortable going back into the Kauffman household made her.

She crossed the street to the house, stood on the porch, and rang the front doorbell. No answer. Patricia looked around. She could see only portions of the street from the porch; two large evergreen trees grew in front of the walkway to the front door. She tried the bell again; still no answer. She turned, deciding to go around back to try the kitchen door.

She didn't get more than a few steps down the walkway when the sudden, stunning crack came on the back of her head. The night exploded with a thousand stars that had not been there before, and a humming started in her head. Then all was black, and she crumbled to the ground.

Chapter 18

Patricia's eyes fluttered, partly opened, then winced shut at the light. Something pounded outside her head; no, inside. She wasn't sure. She breathed slowly, carefully, concentrated on just her breathing; in, out; in, out. When she was calmly centered on her breathing, she tried to figure out what she could about her surroundings without opening her eyes. The pounding. Stiffness in her neck and back. Hard ridge beneath her back. Birds chirping. The smell of cow shit.

Okay, Patricia thought; I haven't died and gone to hell. No birds singing in hell. I haven't died and gone to heaven. Heaven wouldn't smell like cow shit.

She was somewhere, then, on earth, and she needed to find out where. Patricia opened her eyes, slowly, flinching at the light. She was lying on black metal covered with a thin patina of moisture. She was in the bed of her own truck.

At the realization she sat up too suddenly, and her head began throbbing with red-hot pain, her stomach churning with nausea. Concentrate on the breathing, she told herself. In and out, slowly. In, out.

When she regained her sense of equilibrium, Patricia looked around. She was in the middle of a field, just a few feet off the side of a road. It was early; the sun had not risen far enough to burn off the morning mist and dew. A cow, off to the right of her truck, was placidly and rhythmically chewing on some grass. The cow looked up at her, its wide, brown eyes taking her in.

"You explain it to me, Elsie," Patricia muttered. All she knew for certain right now was that she felt sore and stiff all over. Even the skin on her face felt stiff and sore. She rubbed her face and winced when she touched the skin under her left eye and on her cheekbone. It was tender and swollen.

Patricia pushed her mind back to the day before; the images came slowly. After a long day of work she had been at home, listening to *La Traviata*. Then she had gone to check on Elsa. She remembered the drive to the Kauffmans' home, but she could not remember ever getting there.

She inched her way to the edge of the truck, then after three tries lowered the bed door and slipped over the edge. It took a minute to get herself steady, keep herself standing. She moved slowly to the passenger's side of the truck, leaning on the truck for support. The passenger door was unlocked and open.

Her purse was on the floor on the passenger side. She picked it up and sifted through the items: wallet with credit cards and family photos and cash intact; makeup bag; brush; notepad and ink pen; case of business cards; small bottle of hand lotion.

Keys. That was what was missing. Her key ring was not in the truck's ignition. She opened the zippered pocket of the purse where she kept her spare keys. They were gone. She pawed through the junk on the passenger's side floor. No keys anywhere among the Arby's fast-food bags, old newspaper, carwash slips. The lime-green toy phone caught her eye, and she almost laughed. She wished like hell it worked.

Patricia crossed in front of the truck, intending to get in on the driver's side, press the latch to pop the hood, and try to hot-wire the truck. Then she saw that the truck's two front tires were flat. Keys missing; tires flat, she thought. She hadn't come here, wherever here was, on her own. Someone had brought or forced her here, and whoever it was had wanted her stuck here for a while.

Leaning against the hood of the truck, she looked at the brown-eyed cow.

"Any ideas, Elsie?" Patricia asked. The cow looked at her vacantly, still rhythmically, methodically chewing.

"Sweet St. Peter, I'm talking to a cow," Patricia muttered. She closed her eyes, concentrated on her breathing. In, out; in, out.

After she opened her eyes again, Patricia retrieved her purse from the truck, then moved from the field to the edge of the road. Nothing to the left. She looked to the right and again thought there was nothing; then she saw the distant shape of a farmhouse. She started walking, slowly.

On the other side of the screen door stood a squat woman, clad in a Hawaiian flowered housedress, her salt-and-pepper hair pulled back tautly. She held a spatula and looked like she might use it to swat Patricia away from the door.

"It's kind of early to be selling stuff," the woman said, squinting up at Patricia.

Patricia swallowed painfully; her throat was tight and dry. She smiled, trying to look relaxed and nonthreatening. She felt like she might topple over any minute through the screen door.

"I'm not selling anything, ma'am. It's just my truck broke down just down the road. I'd like to use your phone. I won't be long; I just need to call for help. I'll pay for the call."

The woman's eyes narrowed further. "No need to pay. Miller's Crossing's just up the road a piece. Everything you'd want is there." The woman turned and waddled away. Then she called back, without turning around, "Well, come on if you've got to make the call. I haven't got all day."

Patricia pushed open the screen door, entered, followed the woman through a front room and back to the kitchen.

In the kitchen the woman went to the stove, where she was frying sausages and bacon and eggs. The smell of the fatty grease overwhelmed Patricia, sending a wave of nausea through her. She closed her eyes, trying to steady herself.

"This woman needs to use the phone, Ed."

A man grunted. Patricia opened her eyes and saw the man sitting at the kitchen table, looking at her over a newspaper. His face was gnarled with wrinkles, and he looked as pleased with her presence as his wife did.

"How do you do?" Patricia said faintly. She grasped the back of a chair for support.

The man looked up at her, studying her carefully, and finally smiled, carefully and warily, but not in an unfriendly way. Patricia relaxed a little and smiled back.

"Fine," Ed said. He nodded to the kitchen chair next to him. "Have a seat."

Patricia sat down in the wooden chair slowly. Ed got the phone off the countertop behind him but didn't hand it to her. It was, she noted with surprise, a cordless phone. Farm life goes high tech. She supposed if she'd have been observant on her way through the front room, she'd have noticed a personal computer on a corner desk.

"What happened to you?" Ed asked, sitting back down on his side of the table. He folded up the newspaper and pushed it aside.

"My truck ran out of gas, and I blew a tire. Two tires. I ran off the side of the road just up from your house," Patricia said.

Ed raised his thick, steel-gray eyebrows and ran his hand through his thinning gray hair. "That doesn't explain your bruises."

Patricia wondered just how bad she looked. "I had a—a rough night," she said.

"Hmmph. Yours the black truck?"

"Yes."

"Last night you said you were fine."

"What?"

"Saw you on my way back in from Miller's Crossing. Truck off the road on my land, I figure I ought to check it out. I stopped in the road, rolled down my window, called out, asked if you were okay. You said you were fine."

"I said that?"

Ed looked down at the cordless phone he held, confusion deepening the lines in his face. Whose bad dream is this, wondered Patricia, mine or his? "Come to think of it, I asked if you needed to make a call and you said you had a car phone."

Now Ed was looking up at her in alarm, as if she were potentially dangerous. He glanced at a kitchen drawer, and Patricia figured that was where he kept a gun, or at least a potentially deadly kitchen knife.

She smiled as reassuringly as she could. "Car phone's on the blink."

"I bet she was drunk. Just like Sally. Lots of them like Sally." That was from the woman at the stove.

"It's okay, June," Ed said.

"I wasn't drinking. Just on my way to a—a friend's. I'm not sure I ever got there. Somehow I woke up here this morning, in the back of my truck. I don't recall any of what you told me about last night."

"That's a pretty strange story, lady. Last night you were in the front of your truck, saying you were fine." Ed looked at Patricia carefully. She figured she had a few minutes before he kicked her out.

"It's strange, but it's the truth. I'm Patricia Delaney. Sorry I didn't introduce myself before. I can show you my driver's license if you like—"

"Don't worry about it. You'd best call Ervin's shop in Miller's Crossing. He'll give your truck a tow and get it fixed up: 422-1111. Then if you've been blacking out, you might ought to see Doc Stephenson." Ed handed the phone over to her.

Ed kept talking, but Patricia was no longer listening; his voice dissolved into a distant buzz. The heat and greasy smell of the kitchen closed in on her. She rubbed the back of her neck; it was covered with sweat.

Miller's Crossing, Miller's Crossing, Patricia thought, they both mentioned that name. Of course, the town near the Blue Bird Motel. Somehow, someone had brought her—forced her?—to come back to the town in Kentucky where Andy had been murdered.

The realization made her head spin. Suddenly the room went black, and Patricia pitched forward on the kitchen table.

Chapter 19

As Patricia came to again she tried to stretch and felt something tug at the inside of her right arm. She opened her eyes gradually to dim light and slowly assessed that she was in a bed in a quiet room, with an IV attached to her arm. Hospital, she thought. She closed her eyes, letting the realization sink in. She hated hospitals.

Slowly Patricia opened her eyes again and heard a rustling to her left. A young woman sat in a chair by the bed, busily sketching or writing on a large pad of paper.

The young woman looked up at her, saw she was awake, then smiled. "Hi. About time you woke up."

"Lucy?" She sounded like Lucy, but other than the shock of dyed jet-black hair, she didn't look like her. This young woman's face was scrubbed, and she wore a plain pink T-shirt and jeans. Her hair was pulled back in a simple ponytail.

The young woman smiled encouragingly. "How are you feeling?"

Patricia stared at her. "Lucy?"

"Yes?"

"You look funny."

"Thanks. You don't look so hot yourself."

Patricia struggled to sit up. Lucy put her drawing pad and pencil on the floor and helped Patricia. "Take it easy," she said. "You're going to feel faint."

Patricia relaxed against the pillows. "Yeah," she said, willing the throbbing in her head to go away. "Okay. Give me all the usual crap. Where am I? How'd I get here? When can I get out? And what the hell happened to you?''

Lucy laughed. ''Welcome back, Auntie Patricia. Now I know you're going to be okay.''

Patricia grimaced. ''That's comforting. Can you get me some water?''

''Let me call a nurse—they'll want to know you're awake.''

Patricia protested, but Lucy buzzed for a nurse anyway. Two nurses came, checked her IV, rearranged her pillows, and gave her some ice chips, which they then took away before she could gobble them all down.

When they had gone, Patricia gave Lucy a dirty look. ''Was that entirely necessary?''

''What?''

''Calling the nurses?''

Lucy rolled her eyes. ''Give me a break. You're in here for a mild concussion, you've been in and out all night, and you're going to give me shit for calling the nurses when you come to?''

''They took my ice away.''

''If you're going to pout, I'm not staying. And I'm not answering your questions.''

''Okay, fine. How long did you say I've been out?''

''Overnight.''

''Sweet St. Peter. And I've got a concussion?''

''Mild one, but yeah. You can probably go home tomorrow afternoon.''

''What is this, Thursday morning?''

''Friday morning.''

Patricia took a deep breath and slowly let it out again. ''Friday morning. Okay. This explains this weird dream I had about this field where my truck was—and this farm couple—''

Lucy smiled. ''Not a dream, Auntie dear. It was the couple—the Binders—that called an ambulance for you after you passed out on their kitchen table. At least Mr. Binder did.''

''How did you know this?''

''I've been here about since you've been here. Got a phone

call from the hospital right after you were admitted. Dean drove me down.''

"You've been here all this time?''

Lucy looked away. "Yeah, well, you don't keep anything to eat in the fridge, and I'd finished off the white chocolate mousse cake. I figured here I'd get some food. Even if it is crummy hospital stuff.''

Patricia smiled. "Okay. I was afraid you were growing mushy on me.''

Lucy looked back at her and scowled, but the effect wasn't quite the same without her heavy purple makeup. "Someone had to keep Dean company. He was worried about you. He had to go back up to Alliston this morning, but he'll be back tonight.''

"Where the hell am I anyway?''

"Good Samaritan in Miller's Crossing.''

"I guess I owe Mr. Binder a thank-you for that.''

"He seemed like a nice enough old dude,'' Lucy said. "Came up here a few hours after you were admitted. Worried about you. I guess he's not used to women trashing their trucks in his field then passing out in his kitchen. He was concerned. Said you kind of reminded him of their daughter, Sally. Sally was killed in a car wreck a few years ago.''

"Sounds like you had quite a talk with him yourself.''

Lucy shrugged. "He was a nice old guy. Kind of lonely.''

You too, thought Patricia. The Lucy who came in on the Greyhound a few weeks ago would have written Mr. Binder off as an old, worthless man, not cool enough, or hip enough, or whatever the term was these days, to merit consideration.

"He told me the night before I came to in his field he'd seen me in the truck, and that I said everything was okay. I don't remember that at all.''

"Part of the concussion. The doctors said you wouldn't remember what happened before you were knocked out.''

Patricia looked sharply at Lucy. "Knocked out, huh? Is that what happened?''

Lucy nodded. "That's what they think happened.''

"Who's they?''

"The doctors. And the cops."

"The cops?"

"Yeah. I got worried when you were gone all night. The next afternoon I called Dean at the tavern. He didn't know where you were. We went to the office; you weren't there. So we called the police. Turned out they were looking for you anyway."

"Why?"

"They'd gotten another call—an emergency at one of your client's homes—"

"Elsa!"

"Yeah, that's right. Elsa Kauffman."

"I was on my way to see her, but I don't remember ever getting to her house."

"A neighbor had gone over to check on Elsa—something they'd been doing since her father died. Front door was unlocked and open. They found her dead—overdose of tranquilizers."

Patricia stared at Lucy, stunned, unable to find words to match her sudden sense of panic.

"There's more, Patricia. Report in the newspaper yesterday said that she'd written a suicide letter confessing she'd killed her father, and an Andy something or other."

Patricia stared up at the ceiling, forced herself to calm down. "Sweet St. Peter," she whispered. Her throat felt dry.

"Do—do you want me to call the nurses again?"

"No! No—I—" Patricia paused and tried to get comfortable. "I'm okay. It's just—that's not what happened. I can't believe Elsa did that."

"The police seem pretty convinced from what the papers say."

"Yeah, well—I don't believe it. Elsa couldn't have done any of that."

"All kinds of people kill other people."

"Yeah. And I might believe she killed her father—even Elsa could have been driven to it. Maybe especially someone like Elsa. But that doesn't explain why I was knocked out, what the hatpins are supposed to mean, even the missing money—somehow this all has to be connected—''

"Maybe I'd better call the nurse.''

Patricia half laughed. "I'm babbling, huh? That's okay. None of it made sense before this concussion, either.''

"Maybe that's not what happened, like you say." Lucy picked up her sketch pad. "But I was still really worried.''

"Afraid to lose your auntie to a nutcake?''

Lucy looked up, her face pinched and serious. Her mouth was puckered, and Patricia was surprised to see that her eyes glistened. "Yeah, I guess. You—you're the first person who seemed to give a damn about me just for my sake in a long time.''

"I wasn't very nice—''

"No. But I didn't need nice.''

"Sounds like you've done some thinking.''

Lucy nodded. "I have, especially in the last few days. I thought about what you said, about me having to do what I want. I—I had a long talk with Mr. Binder about everything last night. In the cafeteria.''

"What did he say?''

Lucy shrugged. "Not much. He just listened. But it helped me decide what to do.''

Patricia looked at Lucy and studied her scrubbed clean face, surprised that it looked so young while her eyes looked so old and tired. She reached out, pushed a strand of the wiry black hair away from Lucy's brow.

"I won't ask you to tell me what you've decided. But I'll be glad to listen.''

Lucy looked away, unsuccessfully fighting back tears. "I'm not going back to Mom's, except to get my things. I guess I love her, but I can't stand to be around her scene anymore. I've already called a friend; I can stay with her family this coming school year so I can graduate from high school. Then next fall I guess I'll try to go to school. Study art.''

"Art?'' Patricia never knew Lucy was interested in art.

"Yeah. Art. Graphic art. Maybe fine art. I don't know. I

figure it's the one thing I can kind of do. I haven't put a pencil to paper for years, until the past few weeks. Dean bought me the paper. Nice guy, huh?''

Lucy put the sketch pad on Patricia's lap. Patricia picked it up, looked at the sheet, and was amazed at what she saw. The sketch was of her kneeling down, with Sammie standing in front of her. The drawing offered more than just an accurate likeness of Patricia and her dog. It conveyed a sense of motion, of time, a moment caught—she had just knelt down, and smiled, and started to pet Sammie, while he was starting to look up at her, and behind her the trees were caught in midmotion in the wind. Her expression was happy, carefree, enjoying the moment.

Patricia looked up, tears blurring her eyes. "This is—this is—''

"Stop it. I figured you deserved something for putting up with me for these past weeks.''

"Look—if you need some more time before you go back to Maureen's—''

"Thanks. But I'm going to visit Gramps and Grandma.''

"Mom? And Dad? In Maine?''

"Yeah. I figure I might as well get to know them again. I have some memories of them, but not a lot.''

"You sound like you already called and made the arrangements.''

"Yeah. With Grandpa. He sounded nice enough.''

"He's not. He's like me.''

"Thanks for the warning.''

Patricia rubbed her eyes. "Any more surprises?''

"Yeah. I'm letting my hair grow out. What do you think?''

"I think you'll be the only kid in school next year with blond roots.''

They both laughed at that. After the laughter died down, they shared a moment of silence. It was enough for each of them to know they'd reached a truce.

The moment passed, and Lucy picked up the drawing. "I signed it,'' she said. She propped it up on the table next to the bed so Patricia could still see it. "Do you want me to ask the nurses if you can have more ice?"

Patricia shook her head. "Nah. I'm just tired."

"Okay. I'll get out of here and let you get some rest." Lucy paused, and bit her lip. "Uh, Patricia, there's something else. I, uh, found this." She reached into her pocket and pulled out Patricia's gold necklace, with the treble-clef amulet. She handed it to Patricia then sighed. "No—I didn't find it. I—I took it. I'm—sorry—Aunt Patricia."

Patricia looked at the necklace, then closed her fist over it. She nodded. "Apology accepted."

Lucy smiled briefly, then turned and left, shutting the door behind her.

Patricia moved back down in the bed under the covers and looked at the drawing of herself with Sammie, contentedly kneeling at the edge of a forest. She kept looking at the drawing until she fell asleep, still clasping the necklace, then dreamed of a long walk in the woods with Sammie, a long, contented walk because somehow she had figured out something important about the Kauffman family, so that finally the past few weeks made sense to her.

Chapter 20

The interrogation room was cramped and small, the chairs, table, and walls all a grayish off-white. It was designed to make people want to escape it, and the only way to get out of there was to answer the police officer's questions satisfactorily.

That Patricia had done. She had given her statement to Detective John Derrick—and it had been brief—about what happened the night she went to the Kauffman house.

Derrick seemed satisfied. He smiled stiffly. "Thanks for coming in so quickly, Ms. Delaney. We didn't expect you this soon, but your statement can help us wrap up this case."

Patricia leaned back in her chair, crossed her arms, and looked directly at the detective. Despite the clear indication that she could leave, despite the discomfort of the room, she had no intention of leaving.

Derrick frowned and said, "I'll be happy to show you out, Ms. Delaney."

Patricia remained seated and didn't say anything. Her behavior was out of character for a witness in an interrogation room, and though Derrick was too well controlled, too experienced to let it show, he was uncomfortable with her. The detective, she thought, who held himself with a strongly authoritative, self-possessed air, was used to getting and keeping the upper hand. When they first entered the room, he had let her pick one chair, then directed her to the other. She imagined he did that with every witness to establish his authority subtly but clearly.

She smiled and said quietly, "I'm not done with my statement."

"What would you like to add, Ms. Delaney?"

"Elsa didn't do it. She didn't kill her father, and she didn't kill herself."

"Do you have any proof you'd like to share with us of who did kill her father—and her, then?"

"No. But I know she didn't do it. Look—I realize she was missing for hours the night her father was killed, but I know she wasn't capable of premeditated murder."

Derrick tilted his head to one side. He was patronizing her, not really interested, thought Patricia. "Why not?"

"Because I know Elsa. Kill her father in a moment of passion—maybe. I could see Friedrich driving her to that."

"Why?"

"He controlled her. She lived under his thumb for all of her life. It's possible for anyone, no matter how low their self-esteem, to finally find a kernel of self-worth, get angry about the wasted life, and blow someone away in anger for that, maybe during a confrontation of some kind."

"And you don't think that happened."

"Of course not! And you know it didn't, too!" Patricia leaned back in her chair, bit her lower lip, wishing immediately she hadn't raised her voice. Derrick, with his cool calm exterior and dissecting bright eyes, still had control of this conversation, whatever she would prefer to think. Fine, she thought, so be it. I can still get my point across.

She took a deep breath. "Look. When I went to the Kauffmans', I was knocked out, I was driven across the state line and apparently knocked out again, and my truck was purposefully incapacitated. My keys were taken and the truck tires slashed. Someone wanted me out of the way purposely."

"And you don't think Elsa Kauffman was capable of doing all this?" Elsa's suicide note had explained that she had wanted Patricia out of the way in case she figured out the truth and went to the authorities before Elsa herself could write her confession and kill herself. That did not make sense to Patricia.

"No, I don't. There is a mind behind all of this, carefully plotting or planning, someone who wants Elsa to take the blame for murdering Friedrich. Elsa wouldn't have planned something this elaborate, this carefully, and if she had, she wouldn't have had the spirit to see it through."

Derrick leaned across the table and looked evenly at Patricia. "Do you want to know what I think? I think, Ms. Delaney, that you don't like the idea that someone like Elsa used you. She had to hire you anyway to find Andy and the missing money and decided to set up the hatpin notes as a ruse, perhaps use you later as a witness that there had been an outside threat. Then later she realized the ruse wouldn't work, we were onto her, and she killed herself." He paused to smile. "You don't like that scenario very much, do you?"

"Do you really believe that's what happened?"

"Yes."

"Your theory doesn't explain Andy Lawson's murder," Patricia added.

Derrick frowned. "I don't see how that enters into this. The police department in Miller's Crossing has concluded that he was the victim of robbery. Probably flashed some of the money around he took from the Kauffmans, got followed back to the motel, and there you have it."

Except, thought Patricia, that she was fairly sure that Brenda and Tom, not Andy, had taken the money. She decided not to mention that.

"Your theory doesn't explain why the hatpins had been purchased and the motel room reserved under the Jack Grierson name. Don't you find that interesting at all? Personally I think the Miller's Crossing police are taking the easy way out by saying Andy was robbed. No one can even be sure it was Andy in that room the whole time—no one got a good look at anyone in that room. They only saw Andy after he was murdered."

"The Andy Lawson case is out of my jurisdiction, you know that. And as for the false name—maybe Elsa got Andy to purchase the hatpins for her. Maybe his payoff was the hundred thousand and they were working together."

"Next you're going to suggest Elsa killed Andy to cover up his involvement."

Derrick tilted his head to the side, cocked an eyebrow, and grinned at her. "Hmm. Interesting angle. Thank you, Ms. Delaney, we really hadn't considered that."

"I'm telling you that there's one mind behind this—it all has to connect somehow—one solitary mind manipulating all of it—the hatpins, Andy's death, and Friedrich's and Elsa's, and knocking me out, and you want to make a joke out of it!"

Derrick sat up very straight. He was no longer smiling. "Let me tell you something, Ms. Delaney. I see this a different way. I see a woman who was tired of being under her father's thumb, as you yourself put it, who did come up with an elaborate plan to murder her father, and who felt overwhelmed by guilt at the end and killed herself. And I see a private eye—or what is it you call yourself?—an investigative consultant, who got out of her league, who got used by the desperate woman as part of her plan, who got set up, and who can't admit it to herself, or anyone else."

Patricia took a deep breath, trying to calm down. She was sweating. Anger knotted her stomach and throat. "Is that all?" she asked hoarsely.

"No. I'm in charge of this case, and I don't need your help. The Miller's Crossing police don't need your help either. You have no more right than any other citizen to interfere in police business. Understand?"

"I understand."

Detective John Derrick stood up, opened the door, and led Patricia out of the interrogation room.

Dean was waiting for Patricia outside of the police station in his restored baby-blue '76 Camero. She put on her sunglasses, crossed the parking lot in the intense midday heat, and got in the car, slamming the door shut. She closed her eyes and concentrated on the cool air-conditioning, the country-and-western music playing on the radio.

"How did it go?" Dean asked.

"Like hell."

"You don't appear too beat up. They couldn't have roughed you up that badly. And they did let you out."

"Very funny, Dean. Let's just get out of here, okay? I want to get home, drink some iced coffee, heavy on the bourbon, and take a bubble bath and a nap."

Dean snapped off the radio, pulled out of the parking lot and into the traffic. Patricia kept her eyes shut and dozed off, letting the silence and the cool air lull her to sleep.

Suddenly she started awake, her heart and mind racing. She pulled off her sunglasses and looked outside—green heavy trees, bright sunlight; they were on a country road.

"Where are we? Where—"

"Hey—you're okay." Dean reached over and patted her leg. "We're on the way to your place. Almost there. You must have had a bad dream."

Patricia settled down in the seat again, trying to relax and recall the dream. In the dream in the hospital she had been contented, walking with Sammie in the woods, because she had finally figured out what had happened in the Kauffman family. In this one she had been in the woods again, running alone, terrified, hearing Elsa's voice in her ear—even though Elsa was nowhere to be seen—whispering to her, horror stories about her family and her father that made it all seem to make sense, made the running—from or to something?—necessary. Now Patricia could not recall any of Elsa's words.

Soon Dean pulled into the lane to the Carswells' house and drove past it down to the carriage house Patricia rented. Her Chevy S-10 was parked by the carriage house, polished to a shining deep jet black.

"My truck! I thought you said the shop you had it towed to wouldn't be done for two more days!"

Dean pulled up alongside the truck and stopped the Camero, then leaned over and turned Patricia's face toward him. He kissed her lightly on the lips.

"I lied. I wanted to surprise you. I threw in a few extra bucks to make sure they'd get it done before any of their other jobs. Much as I'd enjoy chaperoning you around, I know you'd hate it. You don't like to be tied to anyone, do you?"

Patricia smiled, knowing he already knew the answer to that. "Dean—I'm sorry I was kind of rough outside the police station. It's just—"

Dean kissed her again, then let go of her chin. "Forget it. Get out of here and go look at your truck."

Patricia got out of the Camero and ran over to her truck. New tires. Polished to a mirrorlike finish. She opened the door and looked inside; it was clean, too, even smelled clean. No trash on the floor, but the lime-green toy phone was sitting on the passenger's seat. For a second she considered throwing it out. Then she changed her mind, grinning at the toy and the silly joke it represented. Maybe she'd think of it as a good-luck charm. Her attacker could have killed her, but hadn't. She'd keep the phone in the truck as a reminder of how lucky she was to be alive, her first acknowledgment of the possibility of fate.

She shut the door and turned. Dean stood right behind her, grinning.

"You're like a kid at Christmas."

"Dean, you didn't have to go to this much trouble—"

"Hush. I wanted to. A welcome-back-I'm-glad-you're-okay gift."

Patricia grinned. "Thanks."

"You're welcome. You going to ask me in for a beer, or what?"

"Sure, c'mon."

Patricia opened the front door to her home, expecting Sammie to come bounding up to her, and perhaps Lucy to say hello.

Instead, the second she opened the door, she heard loud music. Jay Bell and the Queen River Band stood in the middle of her family room, playing a rock-and-roll version of "For She's Jolly Good Fellow." Lucy and other friends were clapping along more or less in time and grinning at her. By the time the song was finished, everyone had dissolved in laughter.

The party broke up two hours later. When everyone had left but Dean, Patricia collapsed on a couch and looked up at Dean and Lucy.

"You two . . ." she said.

They looked at each other with exaggerated innocence. "Us?" said Dean. "What did we do?"

"Planned all this." Patricia gestured toward the room, indicating the leftover bowls of chips and snacks, beer bottles, glasses.

"Nah. We had a party like this every day while you were gone," said Lucy.

"Not quite the bubble bath and nap you wanted," Dean said. "But I hope you didn't mind."

"No. It was fun. Took my mind off of things. Thanks, you two," Patricia looked around the room. "But now it appears the party's over. I'd better clean this up—"

"We'll do it," said Lucy. "Why don't you take your bath and nap?"

"Okay. I'll go over my mail first, then to bath and bed."

Patricia went over to her desk while Lucy and Dean started cleaning up. She picked up the pile of mail and began sifting through it. A bill, another bill, coupons she didn't want and wouldn't use, more junk mail, a lingerie catalog, *Harper's* and *Opera News* magazines—she put those aside, she could read them in the tub—a letter from her mother—that went with the magazines—an envelope with just her name on it, another bill. . . .

She stopped and backed up to the envelope. Her name was pasted on in front, spelled out in letters cut from the newspaper. She stared at it a minute, her heart pounding, her right hand rising automatically to rub the scar on her chin. Slowly she turned the envelope over, examining it. No postmark. Nothing but her name in newsprint on the front. She opened the envelope slowly.

A hatpin fell out. This one was a pink gold-carved rose. A note was skewered on the end.

Patricia picked up the hatpin, slid the note off, and opened it. Its message was simple, and also cut from the newspaper. *Guess who?* it said.

Patricia held the hatpin in the palm of her hand. "Lucy?" she said. Her voice cracked on the name.

Lucy came over, stood beside her. "Yeah? Hey, what's that?"

Patricia picked up the envelope, handed it to Lucy. "When did this come? Do you remember?"

Lucy shrugged. "No, I don't. I just gathered up the mail and put in on your desk with the mail that was already there—I didn't pay attention to what you got. Hey—are you okay?"

"Fine."

"You look a little pale—"

"No, I'm fine." Patricia smiled quickly and took the envelope back from Lucy and dropped the hatpin in. "I'm going to take that bubble bath now."

"What is that anyway?"

"Nothing important. A—gift. From an acquaintance."

Lucy went back to join Dean in the kitchenette.

Patricia stared at her name on the envelope. The hatpin was from someone who knew her, a taunting invitation to find out who that someone was.

It wasn't just good luck that her assailant hadn't killed her, Patricia realized. Whoever had knocked her out—the same person, she was certain, who had killed Elsa, and Friedrich, and Andy—wanted her alive. For some reason, the person wanted her to know that he or she was watching her, waiting for her to find him or her.

Patricia took a deep breath and considered her options. She could ignore the hatpin message and wait to see what would happen next. No, too dangerous. She could go to the police. No, probably pointless. Since Lucy couldn't place when the hatpin came, there was nothing to prove that Elsa had not left it. Patricia hadn't checked her mail the night she'd gone to check on Elsa. The police wouldn't take this as evidence that she was right about Elsa, no matter how certain she felt that she was.

She, alone, had to deal with this.

Patricia put the envelope with the hatpin in her briefcase. Tomorrow, after taking Lucy to the Greyhound bus station, she'd get back to work and find the answer to the hatpin's taunting question.

Chapter 21

Patricia and Lucy sat beside each other on the hard plastic seats in the Greyhound bus station in Cincinnati, waiting for Lucy's bus to arrive to take her back to Detroit. About fifteen other people were also waiting restlessly.

Lucy was nervous. She bit her lip and kept playing with the silver cross around her neck. She had on the same outfit she had arrived in, but with her hair back in a ponytail and no makeup, she no longer looked like the nun from hell.

"Wondering what to say to your mom first?" Patricia asked.

"Wondering what to say to her at all," Lucy said, half smiling

"She still doesn't know you're going to Mom and Dad's?"

"No. She'll throw a fit, especially since last night when I talked to her it sounded like things had gone rotten with her and Rick."

"How long before you get in to Detroit?" Patricia asked. She knew the answer; she'd asked the question twice already on the way to the station. She was just running out of things to say, and she didn't know how to tell Lucy to take care of herself, to give her a call sometime, without suddenly sounding mushy.

"About four and a half hours. I guess this is the route where you go through every hick town between here and Toledo."

"I put something in your duffel bag that will help you survive the ride."

"What?"

159

"In your duffel bag. Open it up and see."

Lucy gave Patricia a quizzical look.

"Go ahead, take a look. I'm not going to tell you what it is."

Lucy picked up the battered duffel bag and opened it. For a minute she just stared at the small sketch pad and the box of charcoals, like she had discovered the results of a miracle nestled on top of her wadded-up T-shirts and lingerie.

She looked up at Patricia with shining eyes and a quivering smile. "How did you get these in here after I packed?"

"While you were saying good-bye to Sammie."

"Patricia, you didn't have to—"

Patricia cut off the comment with a shrug. "I wanted to."

Lucy's quivering mouth broke into a full-fledged grin. "You always do what you want to."

Patricia grinned back. "I try."

The announcement for the bus to Detroit came in over the loudspeaker, scratchy and garbled, but still audible. Lucy shut the duffel bag, slung it over her shoulder, and stood up. Patricia stood, too, and for a minute they just looked away from each other, Patricia at the people slowly heading for the door leading out to the buses, Lucy down at her suitcase.

"Hey, give me a call—" started Patricia.

"Call me at Grandfather's—" Lucy started at the same time.

They both laughed, and looked away from each other awkwardly.

"Oh, sweet St. Peter," Patricia said. "Come here, kiddo."

Patricia and Lucy embraced for just a few seconds. When they separated, Patricia said, "Go on. You haven't heard the last from Auntie Patricia."

Lucy smiled. "Good," she said softly.

She turned suddenly and walked off with the other passengers through the double door to the bus without looking back. Patricia watched until Lucy was gone, and watched for a few minutes after that, until it was just her and two old men in the corner in the station.

Then she turned and headed outside, back to her truck, back to the overly bright day, back to her own set of decisions to face. First she was going back to her office, to start the research she knew she needed to do. Then she was headed to the Lucky Clover Diner in Miller's Crossing, where she hoped the trucker Randy Finster could give her something, anything to help her identify who had stayed at the Blue Bird Motel using Jack Grierson's name.

After three hours sitting in the hard seat of the booth in the Lucky Clover Diner, Patricia felt as though she'd never been anywhere else in her life. Surely she had always been staring at a green-and-white tablecloth and an old Coca-Cola bottle filled with yellow plastic daisies and green four-leaf clovers, thick with dust. Surely she had always sat here just like this, her rear end numb, her lower back aching, her head throbbing from too much caffeine.

Surely she had always sat here, listening to the rhythmic turning of the ceiling fan, to the bell when the door opened, to the conversations behind and around her—the little buzzings about who said what at the Baptist church's Chili Cook-off about that nice Deacon Jones and Mrs. Carpenter, about Millie's husband going off again, about how much Louis and Jake spent on their last vacation to Hong Kong. Surely she had always sat here, watching the comings and goings of people: of families; of older ladies who were lifelong friends but looked enough alike by now to be mistaken for sisters; of working men, hard and grizzly and greasy; of chatty teenagers giggling and guffawing at themselves and everyone else. Surely she had always been here, just like this. Sure she had. Always had; always would.

Betty came over, topped off Patricia's cup with coffee, put a hand on her hip.

"You sure you don't want something? Pie, maybe. We got banana cream—"

"Thanks no. You're sure Randy will come through here tonight?" Patricia asked.

"Always in on Monday and Thursday night, like clockwork. He likes my banana cream pie," Betty said, and winked, making it sound faintly obscene. " 'Course, there's no accounting for weather, or flat tires, or being sick."

"Right. Thanks, Betty."

"You know, I ain't never seen anyone so persistent," Betty said, then flounced off in her green-and-white waitress dress.

After dropping Lucy off at the Greyhound bus station, Patricia had gone to her office. She rearranged the meetings she had missed while in the hospital and for the coming week. Then she went through everything in the Kauffman files, every note, every possibility, every bit of concrete information.

Patricia had also called her family friend John Weaver, to see what was taking so long in getting the rosters of the army company Jack Grierson had served in. Bureaucracy, he said. She explained the urgency as clearly as she could without going into too many details. He promised he'd try to speed up the search as much as possible.

Then she'd started her research on Leroy Hibberd before coming down here to—she hoped—meet Randy Finster.

For the past three hours of sitting, waiting for Randy to show up, Patricia had turned over in her mind the pieces that she had, trying to get some of them to fit so she could get enough of a picture to fill in the rest herself. Tom and Brenda had actually taken the money; it was possible that Friedrich had found out, a fight ensued, and one of them had killed him. But why the hatpin notes? Those suggested a plan, a need to frighten Friedrich. The hatpins had been Friedrich's mother's, so it was logical to assume that the need to threaten was connected in some way to the Kauffman family.

Elsa had claimed to remember nothing about them, and that was plausible since she was the youngest of the three children. Brenda could have remembered them, bought them after the auction, using the name of someone she or Tom had known. Perhaps her plan had been to frighten, then blackmail, her father, using the money to finance her and Tom's schemes. Tom was old enough to have served in the Vietnam

War and could have made friends with a Jack Grierson; Brenda could have known a Jack Grierson back then, too.

Henry was also old enough to have served in the Vietnam War and been buddies with Jack. He had also been gone for the weeks during which his father had been getting the threatening notes. Had he actually stayed down here, delivering the notes, then confronting his father? Patricia could not identify a motive for him, but then she was sure she would not understand the motive, the taunting message of the hatpins, the need to murder with one of the hatpins, until she knew who had killed Friedrich. For now she was concentrating on Brenda, Tom, or Henry—or some combination. She had not told Henry what she had learned about Brenda and Tom, and would not until she was sure he was not Friedrich's murderer.

As for Andy and Elsa, each of them had crossed the path of the murderer and had died for the mistake. Elsa had found something in the Kauffman home that made her realize who had killed her father. Andy—that was tougher to figure out. Perhaps, as Detective Derrick had suggested, Andy had been working in league with the killer, staying at the motel while he delivered the hatpin notes. Or perhaps he had not stayed there at all but had in some other way crossed the killer's path.

Patricia had plenty of time to decide what to do if the trucker, the roster of Grierson's mates, or for that matter, Leroy Hibberd were unable to point her in the direction of the killer. She would slowly crawl over every scrap of information she could find about Freidrich's life. Something in his life, something that had happened or that he had caused to happen, would explain the hatpins and what they signified, and that would be the key to finding his, Andy's, and Elsa's killer.

A shadow fell across the table. Patricia looked away from the window and up at a man. He wasn't very tall, square built, wearing a blue short-sleeved shirt, blue jeans, boots, and a belt with a buckle big enough to hold the Lucky Clover's blue-plate special.

"Randy Finster?"

The man studied Patricia for a second, sizing her up. "Betty said you wanted to talk to me."

"I do," she said, and nodded at the empty seat across from her.

Randy slid into the seat, placed his folded hands on the table. He looked at Patricia, waiting, his charcoal eyes tired but otherwise unemotional, ringed with deeply etched lines and overshadowed by bushy eyebrows. His gray-and-black crew-cut hair wasn't much longer than the stubble on his jaw and chin. His was a beefy face with heavy jowls that gave him a weighed-down, tired look, that might have made him look slow, except for the reserved intelligence in his eyes. This was a man who had seen and heard a lot, Patricia thought, and who was practiced at revealing very little. Randy wasn't going to tell her anything until he knew exactly what she wanted, and decided, on his own terms, that helping her out was worthwhile.

Patricia pulled a business card out of her purse and put it on the table before him. He glanced at it without picking it up.

"Investigative consultant," he said.

"Yes."

"Consultant. I don't like that word."

"A lot of my clients do. Private investigator scares them. It just means I help people find out things they need to know."

"I know what it means. It usually means hatchet man, or con. Who decides?"

"Decides what?"

"If these people need to know."

"They do. I just get the information for them."

Randy got out a cigarette, lit it, and squinted at her through the haze of his smoke. "You're a highly paid snitch."

Patricia grinned. "I'm an okay paid snitch."

Randy took a drag on his cigarette. "At least you don't take yourself too seriously."

"No. But I take getting information for my clients seriously. And I need to ask you a few questions."

Randy just looked at her.

"There's a man you talked with a few times in here."

"I talk with a lot of people."

"This one went by the name Jack Grierson. Wore a hat, sunglasses all the time. Didn't talk to anybody much while he was in town, except, according to Betty, you."

"Yeah, so? If you're after him on behalf of his old lady, I don't get involved in that stuff. People's personal lives are their own business."

"I'm after him because I think he killed three people. And I think he may be trying to kill me."

Randy froze with his cigarette partway to his lips. Then his arm sank slowly and he stubbed the cigarette out. He whistled softly.

"Jesus. You're sure as shit straightforward, lady." His voice held a little more respect, and Patricia knew he'd talk with her now. Before coming to meet him, she'd run a computer check on him. He was a family man—wife and three kids in Memphis, living in a decent, lower-middle-class neighborhood. He'd been a welder, and a spokesman for the unionized employees at his company during a strike for better pay, benefits, and fair treatment from company management. When corruption in the local union at a different company was discovered during the strike, he was outspoken and outraged in the local papers. The AP newswire had carried the stories. Apparently since then he'd decided he had had enough and drove his own rig. Patricia could appreciate that.

"Look, you want to order your dinner now, before we talk?"

"Yeah. Yeah, I guess so."

Betty came by a few minutes later, took Randy's order for chicken pot pie and mashed potatoes, then topped off Patricia's coffee and poured Randy a cup.

"Food here's a lot better than the truck stop up the road," he said.

"Betty tells me you're in here on Monday and Thursday nights."

Randy nodded.

"Which night was it when Jack approached you?"

Randy lit another cigarette, squinted his eyes, thinking. "Monday," he said finally. "I had finished eating, was playing a few arcade games. He came over, asked if I minded some company. I didn't really care one way or another, so he watched me finish the game, then we sat down. He said he'd seen me get out of my rig; was I going through Cinci. I said yeah, he asked if I'd give him a lift, and I said sure. Seemed like a nice enough guy."

"What else did he say? Anything about what he did, why he was here?"

"Naah. Just shot the breeze about sports, mostly. He was a real Reds fan. I figured he was from this area. Talked about football, too." Randy paused to take a drink of coffee. "And Vietnam."

"How did you get on that topic?"

"I guess I brought it up. He wanted to know how I got into trucking. I told him I'd done a lot of driving in Vietnam and, when I decided to get out of welding, thought driving my own rig would be okay. He'd served, too. Worked with explosives."

Patricia's heart clenched; that was the same kind of work the actual Jack Grierson had done. It couldn't have been Andy at the Blue Bird Motel; he would have only been about eight years old at the peak of the war. Andy had not actually stayed at the Blue Bird Motel. Somehow he had just gotten unlucky enough to cross the path of the man who did.

"An Explosive Ordnance Disposal unit?" she asked.

Randy frowned. "Something like that. How did you know?"

Patricia smiled. "I'm an okay paid snitch, remember? Did he say when he'd served?"

"Somewhere between sixty-six and sixty-nine. Mostly we just talked around the war, stayed on the edge of it, you know? He'd lost a buddy in the war, so had I. Nobody talks about it much now, though. We went back to sports."

"Anything else? Did he mention anybody he was seeing here? Anything that stands out from the sports?"

"No, that's about all we talked about. He was pretty interested in hearing about my job, asked a lot of questions about it. Didn't say anything about himself except about 'Nam. I gave him a lift to Cincinnati that night."

"Monday night?"

"Yep, and Thursday."

"I wonder how he got back down here," Patricia mused.

"Didn't say. Another lift, I reckon."

"Where in Cincinnati did you take him?"

Randy shrugged. "Not too sure. I don't know the city real well. He gave the directions and I followed them."

Patricia arched an eyebrow. "Arlington Avenue. Sound right?" It was the cross street to the street where Kauffman's business was located, which was probably too narrow for an eighteen-wheeler.

Randy frowned. "Yep. Sounds right. Yep, that was it."

"He just asked you to drive him there and drop him off, both nights?"

"Yep." He stubbed out his cigarette. "Thursday night he wasn't in here. Just waiting out at my rig when I came out."

So that's how he'd done it, Patricia thought. Stayed in Miller's Crossing, hitchhiked up to Cincinnati to deliver the hatpin messages. Tom or Henry? Either one could have stayed here.

"Was there anything else? Distinguishing scars, tattoos, facial features?"

"No. He kept his hat on the whole time, and sunglasses, and this big blue sweat suit. I thought maybe he'd had cancer therapy, or something, and was trying to hide his bald head or dark eyes or something. So I didn't notice anything—no, wait, there was one thing."

"Yeah?"

"He told this joke one of the nights, when I gave him a lift. Can't remember what it was. But he faked a girl's voice, high-pitched, and then a funny accent. Spanish, I think. I remember thinking he was good with his voice, kind of like some of those comics you see on TV.''

Patricia's throat tightened. The man could change his voice, even make it sound like a woman's. That explained Mr. Binder's confusion. It had been the man, talking like a woman, disguising his voice. In the dark Mr. Binder couldn't tell if a man or woman was in the truck. She shivered. She had been passed out in the back of her truck, she figured.

"Hey, lady, you okay?''

"Yeah, fine. Yes, I'm fine.'' Patricia cleared her throat. "You have my card. Call me if you think of anything else.''

She put down three dollars, to cover the coffee and service for each of the past three hours, then went outside. She stretched, glad to be standing finally. For a minute she just stood, taking in the cooler night air, the husky sound of crickets in the brush around the diner, the occasional firefly in the velvety dark night, the cheery lights of the diner, the neon four-leaf clover buzzing as its light flickered.

Then she started back to her truck. She was almost to her truck when she heard a car start up, an engine race. Kids, she thought, showing off their horsepower. Maybe there wasn't much else to do around Miller's Crossing on a summer night.

Then she was suddenly blinded by the bright lights of the car coming at her.

"Hey, what the—'' she shouted, then started running. The vehicle was heading for her, intending to run her down. She ran as fast as she could, made it to her truck, and hopped on the hood, rolling over it and out of the car's way.

The car spun out of the parking lot and down the road, its lights now out.

Patricia stayed where she was for a few seconds, hunkered down by her truck, breathing hard, heart pounding. That hadn't been a carful of kids, she realized. The car had moved too purposefully toward her, threatening her, then swerving expertly out of the way just before hitting her or her truck. The driver could have easily killed her, but for some reason hadn't wanted to. Just like her assailant several nights before had chosen merely to take her out of commission for a few days instead of killing her.

She stood up and brushed herself off, got in her truck, forcing herself to breathe evenly until she could calm down and safely drive herself home. No, not kids, she thought. Someone, the killer or an accomplice, had followed her here, and had wanted to reinforce the message of the hatpin she had received: she was being watched.

Fine, Patricia thought, fine. Let whoever it was watch her. She was closing in on getting a good look at the hatpin killer.

Chapter 22

Leroy Hibberd's house was built within the last twenty years, a large, sprawling brick ranch on three acres just beyond the suburban outskirts west of Cincinnati. It was not fancy compared with the kind of homes Tom Nielson liked to build, but it was, nevertheless, impressive for a man whose only job since the late 1940s had been as a "consultant" to the Kauffman Agency for an all-time-high salary of twenty-five thousand dollars according to the agency's employees records, along with managing a few of his own apartments. The cash payments of $100,000, logged to overhead, had made a tidy supplement, Patricia supposed—a supplement left unreported to the IRS. Before that, he had worked as a security guard for Friedrich and Russell Knepper when they developed Eagle Rise Estates, Friedrich's only venture into construction with a partner before Tom Nielson came along. That information, along with Hibberd's social security number from his employment records at the agency, had been enough for Patricia to start detailed research on his background, some of it by tapping into databases of real-estate records, some of it by going through records that had yet to become available through a computer.

Patricia opened her truck's door, got out, and started walking up the driveway to Hibberd's front door. No one answered the first few rings of the doorbell, but as she was turning away, about to go back to her truck and wait, the door swung open. A small, older woman stood in the doorway. She had carefully tinted auburn hair, large designer glasses, and wore navy-blue pants and a white blouse that failed to hide the fact that her figure had gone soft. Mrs. Hibberd, Patricia guessed.

"Yes?" she said.

"Hello. I'm Patricia Delaney, and I'm here to see Leroy Hibberd."

Mrs. Hibberd scowled. "I don't think we know you."

"Is Mr. Hibberd in?"

The older woman was about to say something when a man's voice called out, "Who is it, Martha? If it's someone selling something, tell them to get off my property!"

Patricia grinned. "Good, he is here."

"Are you selling something? If so, you heard what my husband said." Mrs. Hibberd started to shut the door.

"No, Mrs. Hibberd, I'm not selling anything. I work for Henry Kauffman."

Mrs. Hibberd looked startled at the Kauffman name and opened the door a little wider. Patricia handed her a business card. "If you give your husband this and tell him I work for Henry Kauffman, I'm sure he'll understand."

Mrs. Hibberd sighed, stepped aside, and gestured for Patricia to come in. "That won't be necessary," she said, giving the card back to Patricia. "Come in."

Patricia stepped in the house, and followed Mrs. Hibberd through an elegant foyer and living room, decorated with cherry and satin furnishings, cut crystal lamps, massive paintings. They stopped at a door to another room.

"My husband is in his den," Mrs. Hibberd said. "I don't think I'll be needed for this discussion. I don't get involved with my husband's business."

She turned and went back through the living room, then disappeared down a hallway.

Patricia went into the den. It took a few seconds to adjust to the contrast with the living room. This room was dark, with wood paneling, black leather furniture, a deer head over the red brick fireplace. Leroy sat in a black leather recliner, feet up, watching a stock-car race on a wide-screen television.

"Martha, did I hear voices? You got rid of that salesman, didn't you?" Leroy called.

Patricia walked over to the couch and sat down. "Not a salesman. Patricia Delaney. I'm an investigative consultant and I work for Henry Kauffman."

For a few seconds Leroy didn't react. He didn't even take his eyes off the wide-screen television. The cars zoomed around another lap on the screen, and then he clicked off the television with a remote control. He looked over at Patricia evenly, assessing her.

"So," he said. "I wondered how long it would be before one of them sent a henchman, after I heard Friedrich died."

Patricia smiled. "Investigative consultant, Mr. Hibberd."

"Nothing for you to investigate here, Miss—what did you say your name was?"

"Patricia."

Leroy narrowed his puffy eyes and peered at her. "Haven't I seen you before somewhere?"

"At an auction a few weeks ago, where Friedrich Kauffman was auctioning off a house and some land. You ran the price up considerably."

Leroy chuckled. "Did I now? Did I? What makes you so sure I didn't want that house for myself?"

"You didn't. You wanted to remind Friedrich that you wanted your hundred thousand."

"Did I now?" Leroy looked suddenly angry. "That was an arrangement between Friedrich and me, just our business."

Patricia resisted a grin. This was the first proof she had that her theory was right, that the cash withdrawals over the years for "overhead" were really going to Leroy, a tidy supplement to his income from the Kauffman Agency over the years.

"Yes, but Friedrich is gone now. And Henry Kauffman, his son, is running the business. If you want your arrangement with the Kauffman family to continue, you'll have to cooperate. I have a few questions—"

"I'll have to cooperate? Will I now?" Leroy was shouting, his face suddenly red and angry. He reared up in his chair. "You go tell Henry that he has to cooperate with me, unless he wants his father's name and his nice little business ruined!"

Leroy clicked the remote, and the cars were zooming around on the big screen again. He stared at them. "And I'm only dealing with Henry."

Patricia was dismissed, she realized, but she stayed on the couch, studying Leroy. The money he had gotten out of Friedrich Kauffman had not made him a happy or pleasant man, she thought. His fleshy face was knotted in a scowl, his mouth twisted in a grimace that only approximated a smile. In his bibbed overalls and working boots, he looked out of place in the leather and mahogany den. She couldn't imagine him in the peach-and-blue living room on the other side of the door. Still, the money, the house, the other toys he'd accumulated over the years were important to him. He wouldn't risk losing them.

Patricia picked up the remote off the end table and clicked off the television.

"What the—" Leroy started.

"Let's get something straight up front, Mr. Hibberd. If you want to keep your arrangement, as you call it, going with Henry Kauffman, you'll answer a few questions. You have been named in Friedrich's will as getting one hundred thousand dollars a year, which I'm sure is no surprise to you. Before Henry decides not to contest the will, he wants to know why you've been named to get that money."

"That money is mine; Friedrich promised it! If Henry tries to keep it from me, I'll ruin his father's name and business!"

"That is a risk," Patricia said, "that Henry is willing to take. He and his father were not close, and he is doing well on his own. You, on the other hand, seem to have come to rely on Friedrich. I don't think you want to lose that."

Leroy sat up straight in his chair, staring at Patricia. He suddenly looked a little nervous.

"This house," Patricia said, "is worth well over two hundred thousand, according to your property records, and is paid for.'' She had quickly learned that through a real-estate database.

"What—you have no right!"

"Oh yes, I do. This is all public information. You also have three restored antique cars, in addition to two newer automobiles, a pleasure boat, a small Cessna airplane, all licensed to your name, all paid for in cash. The interesting thing is that you have listed as your profession 'consultant' and your employer the 'Kauffman Agency' for years, while on the books at the Kauffman Agency you have never been paid more than twenty-five thousand a year. Now, I'm sure you are clever, Mr. Hibberd, but this is rather impressive money management. I find it fascinating that a man who has never made more than twenty-five thousand a year as a consultant has this many assets. I think the Internal Revenue Service would find that interesting, too.''

"You can't—"

"Oh yes, I can. In fact, I'm very good friends with an IRS investigator, and I owe her a favor.'' Patricia was lying about that, but it seemed to scare Leroy. He was licking his lips and rubbing his hands together. "And did you know that Friedrich kept records of all his 'gifts' to you over the years? Double books, one for himself, one for the IRS. His personal books show all that unreported income.''

"He wouldn't have.''

"He did,'' Patricia said. Another lie, and hopefully all it would take to get Leroy to talk about why Friedrich had given him money over the years. "Now, why don't you tell me why Friedrich gave you that money? I can't believe it was just because you were good buddies. Neither does Henry.''

"Henry wouldn't want to get in trouble with the IRS either.''

Patricia shrugged. "Might be cheaper in the long run than paying you a hundred grand for the rest of your life.''

Leroy smiled suddenly, his lips grimacing with a short, nasty laugh. "No, Friedrich and I weren't buddies. But he needed me, oh yes, he needed me to keep quiet, didn't he now? Why don't you ask Henry what he remembers about the Knepper trial? He'd be old enough to remember the trial, I think.''

Leroy's eyes lit up with glee at the look of confusion on Patricia's face. ''Ah, I can see I've surprised you, bringing that up. Let's just say I did some work for Russell Knepper after hours. He was a jealous man and didn't trust his wife, not even with his dear cousin Friedrich. Let's just say I saw some things that put Friedrich in a pretty bad light at the time, and I let Friedrich know it.''

Leroy's smile turned into a snarl. ''It was worth it to him all these years for me to keep what I have—and I have more than just my word for what I saw—hidden away. And it will be to Henry, too. You tell him if he wants to know more, he'll have to come talk to me himself.''

He picked up the remote and brought the stock-car racing back to full speed and volume on his big-screen television. Patricia stood up, let herself out of the house, jumped in her truck, and sped back to her office. She had a murder case from over forty years ago to research.

The entire case, as recorded by the Ohio Court of Appeals, was up on Patricia's computer screen. She had scanned it rapidly first, and now she was reviewing it again, slowly and more carefully. She had gone into a database of legal information, which included state court cases from Ohio, and quickly found what she wanted to know.

On the night of May 3, 1949, Wilma Mae Knepper had been brutally murdered by her husband, Russell Knepper. She had been stabbed repeatedly with a hatpin or perhaps several hatpins. The actual murder weapon had never been found, since all the hatpins were wiped clean of blood and fingerprints, but the hatpins on the dressing table fit her wounds.

There was virtually no doubt that Russell Knepper was the murderer, even though he denied it vehemently and appealed his earlier conviction. Friedrich Kauffman, his cousin and housing-development partner; Leroy Hibberd, a security guard working for Kauffman and Knepper; Scott Mc-

Gregory, the bartender at his favorite bar; Bill and Ethel Graham, his neighbors; and Tony Marcello, his best friend, all regretted to testify that on numerous occasions Russell had accused his wife of being unfaithful to him and had threatened to kill her. In fact, the police had come to his home many times on domestic-disturbance calls.

According to the database information, Russell Knepper had killed his wife and would spend the rest of his life in jail for the crime.

Patricia selected the text of the case to save on her computer. What the judge and jury didn't know, she thought, was that Russell Knepper would end his life early by hanging himself in his jail cell. What they also didn't know was that it was possible, just possible, that one very small boy, about five or six at the time, saw something different from what Russell's peers all said was true, but wouldn't recall it until years later when he went to an auction and saw a collection of hatpins.

Chapter 23

Two hundred and seventy-five names were on the roster that John Weaver had finally sent her for Jack Grierson's army unit from 1967 to 1969. The first name listed was Adams, Edward. Patricia resisted the temptation to jump to the middle of the list where the name she was looking for should be. She had to be careful. She had to read each name individually, breathe deeply, concentrate, take her time.

Deckerson, Cedric. The name she was looking for was Kurt Knepper. Patricia was certain he had known Jack, had been good buddies with him, had chosen to use his name to purchase the hatpins and later to reserve the motel room from which he would deliver his hatpin messages.

Fricker, Hank. What had he seen, or found out later, that had made him want to take his revenge with the hatpins? Somehow Friedrich had been involved with Kurt's mother's murder. Perhaps he had killed her, perhaps he had helped Russell kill her. Whatever the exact truth was, Hibberd had known about it, too, and used it to blackmail Friedrich all these years.

Grierson, Jack. Patricia smiled at the name, with the cursor blinking beside it on her computer, at the silent confirmation that the list was valid. She didn't care about Hibberd just now. She wanted the confirmation that Kurt had known Jack. With that connection tying him firmly to the hatpins and to the motel where Andy was murdered, she was sure she could get the police to help her.

Henderson, Abel. But why would Kurt, assuming she was right, assuming she hadn't overlooked some key fact that pointed to someone else as the killer, want to use a name that would point to him later? Surely he had known that connecting his name to Grierson's would make it tedious, but not impossible, to identify him as the purchaser of the hatpins, as the man who stayed in the room where Andy had been murdered. He could just as easily have made up a name that would be impossible to trace to him.

Johnson, Edward. Simple enough, thought Patricia. Because Kurt had wanted to do more than punish Friedrich. He had wanted revenge. That was the only motive that had made sense all along. Why else the elaborate and bizarre plan of delivering threatening notes on hatpins? Why else kill Friedrich with a hatpin? Revenge was not as sweet, or as satisfying, savored alone.

Knepper, Kurt. Patricia looked at the name on her screen with grim satisfaction and rubbed the scar on her chin.

Elsa had once asked her the most dangerous thing she had ever done. Once it had been to cross a highway overpass hand over hand. Now it would be to confront a murderer. Perhaps it was indefensibly stupid. Perhaps it was too risky. But he had hurt her physically, and worse, he had scared her and shaken her confidence, her trust in the security of her life. She wanted answers, and she wanted to get them from him.

But she wasn't making this crossing without a safety net. First, she had to verify where Kurt was staying. After that, she had to pay a visit to Dean's Tavern. Then she was cashing in on her knowledge about Brenda and Tom's activities.

Brenda opened the door wearing only a negligee with a sheer robe, a carefully made up face, heavy musky perfume, and a smile that faded the minute she registered that it was just Patricia standing at the door.

Patricia shrugged apologetically. "Sorry. It's just me." She held her hands out to show they were empty. "No wine or flowers, either."

"What the hell are you doing here? It's nine o'clock at night!" Brenda said.

Patricia cocked her head. "You appear to have been expecting someone. So at least I didn't waken you."

"I sure wasn't expecting you." Brenda started to close the door.

Patricia grabbed it, held it open. Brenda struggled to finish closing it, gave up, and let the door swing open.

"Okay, so you're stronger than me. Since I can't slam the door in your face, what do you want?"

"To talk to you."

Brenda smiled thinly, just showing the tips of her teeth. Patricia wondered if anyone in the Kauffman family besides Elsa ever gave a genuine smile. "Come in, then. Make it snappy."

Patricia entered in the foyer of the trilevel, glanced at the marble statuette on the cherry half table, reflected in the gold-framed mirror. She followed Brenda into the large, sunken living room.

Patricia sat in a burgundy velvet club chair while Brenda flopped in a burgundy-and-gray-striped satin couch, stuck her feet up on a glass-and-gold table, and lit a cigarette. She took the lid off a cut crystal candy dish and threw her match in the dish.

"Nice room. Nice house," Patricia said.

"Yes."

"This is Oak Villas, isn't it? One of Tom's first developments after taking over his father's company. Is that when you first met Tom, when you and your ex-husband had this house built?"

Brenda took a deep drag off her cigarette, exhaled, watched the smoke rise to the ceiling. "You didn't come here to chitchat. What's your point?"

"Okay, I'll get to the point. You and Tom are more than colleagues. You're lovers."

Brenda cackled. "Brilliant deduction. Tell me, did his little wife, Annie, tell you that?" She exhaled more smoke and watched it rise to the ceiling. "So what. Big deal. Tom's not here now, is he? Probably his little wife has one of her little migraines and he's feeling obligated to stay home with her. The bastard could call.''

She looked up at Patricia, as if suddenly realizing she had been talking to herself. She smiled crookedly. "Don't tell me you came by here to give me a lecture on my scruples."

"I don't care about your affair with Tom. Except that it gave you plenty of time to talk, plenty of time to figure out your plan."

"Our plan."

"Yes. You need Tom, or think you do. Maybe you needed more independence from your father. Tom wanted to finally be in power again, run a business himself. Problem is, the last business he ran, he destroyed. He latched onto you, and your father, as a source of financial backing. Am I getting the picture right so far?"

Brenda didn't say anything, just stared at her, eyes narrowed.

"You just let me know when I get something wrong. You saw the money in the safe. A hundred thousand dollars cash. Not a lot—but enough to get you and Tom starting some deals on the side. I searched a real-estate database and found the property records of the land you bought outside of Columbus, Brenda."

At that Brenda flinched, then quickly tried to recompose herself. "All right. Go on."

"Maybe you figured you could make a go of it, then tell your father to hell with it, I'm out from under your thumb," Patricia said. "Maybe you thought Tom would leave Anne, stay with you, since you're so smart, figuring out how to make him rich and powerful again.

"But there are a couple of problems," she continued. "One, the money is blackmail money your father was paying to someone for years. When the money was gone, your father had to do something about it. It was probably hard enough to come up with that amount about once a year. Enter me, an investigative consultant Elsa hired at your father's orders to find out where the money had gone. Conveniently for you, Andy Lawson turned up missing, so the blame was focused on him. But, of course, we both know he didn't take it. You did.''

Brenda continued looking at her, and Patricia wondered if the woman had even heard her, until she picked up the candy-dish lid and threw it at the chandelier in the corner. The lid hit the target and broke, along with a few crystals from the chandelier, falling like a little ice flurry to the gray carpet.

Brenda looked at Patricia then and smiled, as if she had taken great satisfaction in breaking something. ''You're a bitch, you know that?''

''Thanks.''

Brenda half laughed. ''But then, that's what they always call women who have half a spine. It's funny, I thought I was so smart, coming up with that scheme. And of course, all the records have to be in my name. Tom's name is shit, as far as banks or anyone else in business is concerned.'' She reached up to her eyes and began pulling at her lids. A set of false eyelashes came off. She threw those on the table. ''I don't think Tom is coming, do you?''

''I don't know.''

Brenda leaned forward, reached behind herself, and began fiddling with her back. She undid her bra, then sank back into the couch as if she were quite relieved. Then she lit another cigarette. ''You know, there's chilled champagne and liver pâté in the kitchen if you want some.''

''No, thanks.''

Brenda took a drag off the cigarette. ''It does sound disgusting, doesn't it? At this hour? Pathetic.'' She shook her head, then focused on Patricia again. ''You know, I'm not sure any of this would stand up in court against me. I could deny the whole thing.''

''The records pretty much speak for themselves. And it's enough to convince Henry to cut you out of the business. He has that right under your father's will.''

''I know. My father never really trusted me. And Elsa, the weak one, is the one who killed him. Isn't that funny?'' Brenda gave a half cackle, half laugh at that. Patricia didn't answer.

"I gave up everything to work for my father. I wanted to believe, really believe, the image he and Mother gave us that we were a close family, that this was what a family should be like. I neglected my own family, putting in so many hours for him, hoping to win his approval. Eventually they got tired of it and left me. Don't really blame them."

Brenda sighed and stubbed out her cigarette in the candy dish. "I met Tom at a Christmas party last year for local real-estate brokers. He was trying to get into the business selling. Everyone knew what he'd done, of course, and treated him like a pariah. I remembered him from when we bought this house, and I felt sorry for him. We got to talking that night, and things . . . went from there. I had to beg and plead with Father to take him in as a partner. I think the only reason he did it was because I had been making noises about leaving the family business, and if he gave in to me, he'd just have another way to control me—do this or Tom's out of here."

She laughed, abruptly. "I should have seen my father for what he was years ago—a petty, controlling manipulator. I didn't really see it until Tom was around. And I always thought I was so strong, while poor Elsa was so weak. Dear, dear Elsa. She was the weak, helpless one, and everyone wanted to feel sorry for her. I hated her. Do you know why I hated her?"

"No, I don't," Patricia said quietly.

"Because Daddy always liked her best. I knew it as a kid. I knew it. He made it obvious, that she was better, that I was ugly and stupid compared to her. And then something happened. I don't know what. Suddenly nothing she did was good enough. And he turned on her." Brenda was crying now, her tears and emotion choking her, making her words come out in jerky phrases. "I should have felt sorry for her then, but I kept on hating her, because I was glad for her pain. I was gleeful—now I was the good one. And I hated her, because it was easier to be glad about how he felt about me if I hated her." She wiped her eyes on the back of her hand, smearing mascara on her face and hands. "God, I hate it when I cry."

"It's okay to cry."

"You didn't come by here to play Little Miss Comforter either."

"No, I didn't. I came by because I want something."

Brenda laughed. "Of course. Well, I hope it's not money. I'm fresh out."

"I haven't told Henry what I know. And I won't, if you listen to a little story I want to tell you, and do something for me. Your sister did not kill your father. I know who did."

Brenda's eyes narrowed. "Is this some kind of game?"

Patricia shook her head. "No game. You have a choice. You can hear this story, or I leave here and go tell Henry the one we already know about you and Tom."

Brenda stared down at the broken glass on the carpet that had been her candy-dish lid. She sighed. "That's not much of a choice. Okay. I'll hear your story."

Chapter 24

Patricia sat in the rocking chair in the pink room that had been Elsa's and looked through the photo album. The pictures were typical ones—a pose for Easter, a group shot at Christmas, but like all family photos they told in their own way of more than just the rites of passing time and seasons. The smiles were strained. The poses were stiff and tense, as if no one dared breathe while the pictures were taken. There were no spontaneous pictures of the family on vacation or at play or on a typical day that was not an "occasion." The Kauffman family had gotten the basic, no-frills, standard list of Kodak moments and followed it rigorously for posterity's sake.

The exception was the early photos. These were of Elsa, age seven or eight, dressed up in old-fashioned clothes—her grandmother Gertrude Kauffman's, Patricia guessed. In them, Elsa was posing, but it was a playful, joyous posing. Her childhood face was free of care, shining, smiling, joyful, caught in midgiggle or a delightful attempt to look grown up. She wore the long dresses, the strands of jewels, the big hats, with a grace and freedom particular to children. In one very early shot, Elsa, dressed up, stood with a little boy, two or so years younger, who looked up at her with admiration. In this picture only, there was a hatpin in the hat Elsa wore. The caption below read *Elsa and Kurt, March 1949, at Grandmother Gertrude's House*. The photo must have been what Elsa saw that made her realize who had killed her father.

A year after the 1949 photograph, Kurt was not in any

pictures, and Elsa wore the expression and stance she would wear until her death—rigid, smiling tenuously, eyes wide with fear and bewilderment, shoulders bowed with tension, careful and nervous lest she say or do something inadvertently, inexplicably wrong.

Patricia had come back to the Kauffman house to find this, getting in with a spare key from Brenda. Nothing in the Kauffman Agency had pointed to the killer, so she figured that whatever triggered Elsa's realization of who had killed her father had to be somewhere in the Kauffman house. She remembered the last time she was here that Elsa had been looking at old albums. She also had come here knowing that Kurt was probably still following her. She hoped, if she was right, that she had the time to get the missing pieces of information from Kurt before the police came, assuming Brenda followed her instructions—or before Kurt tried to hurt her.

Patricia heard footsteps coming up the stairs. She stopped rocking, but kept looking at the photos. Breathe in, out. Stay calm, she instructed herself.

The bedroom door opened. Patricia looked up. Kurt stood over her, holding a gun trained steadily on her.

"It was foolish for you to come here," he said. "I've been following you."

"I figured that out on my last visit to Miller's Crossing."

"You should have taken the warning. You should have stayed where you'd be safe."

"I figured from your hatpin message you'd come after me sooner or later."

Kurt sighed and nodded. "Yes. Since you weren't going to back off the case, I had to. Your visit to Hibberd's proved that. You were at Brenda's. What did you tell her?"

"Nothing, except I knew she and Tom had taken the money from the safe."

Kurt laughed, but it was a laugh devoid of humor. It showed he was tired. "Should have guessed those two would be up to something. Where did she go?"

Patricia shrugged. "To meet Tom, I guess." She hoped

her lie hadn't shown in her face. She had told Brenda what she knew, then instructed her to leave just after she did, drive around for forty-five minutes, then go directly to the nearest police station if Patricia hadn't called her on Brenda's car phone. She couldn't be sure Kurt wouldn't go into Brenda's house and hurt her, too. She just hoped, for both her and Brenda's sakes, that Brenda had listened.

"I don't have to 'guess who,' as the hatpin you sent me said, Kurt," said Patricia. "I know you killed Friedrich, Elsa, and Andy. Why Andy had to die, I'm not sure."

Kurt smiled, slowly and sadly. "I suppose this is the part where I'm supposed to confess, then break down in remorse while you call the cops." He shook his head. "It's not going to happen that way." He took a step closer to her.

"I suppose not," Patricia said. "But I still would like to know what happened. I haven't got it all figured out. Just parts of it."

Kurt took a step back, cocked his head to the side. "I wouldn't want to send you to your grave without satisfying your curiosity. Why don't you tell me what you think you know?"

Patricia took a careful breath in, then exhaled slowly, willing herself to stay calm. "Let's start with Elsa. She figured out that you had killed her father. You found out about it and faked her suicide."

"Elsa called me, asked me to come over here, confronted me. A photo in that album you're holding made her remember how I reacted—screaming, then in shock for two days—to the hatpins she was wearing when we were playing dress-up at Great-Aunt Gertrude's house not long after my mother was killed. Then she remembered a night her father came home about the time my mother was killed, and from that pieced some of the story together. Enough to suspect me. You know why she wanted to confront me?"

"No."

"I told you the day you were here after Friedrich's funeral. She admired you. She wanted to be just like you. Brave. And

I guess she was right, you would have confronted me. You're here. Except I don't call it brave. I call it stupid.''

At that, Patricia winced. Her heart clenched and bitter bile rose to her throat. Elsa had imitated how she thought Patricia would act, and now Elsa was dead.

Kurt grunted at her reaction. "I thought you'd like that. Poor little Elsa. Killing her was easy. She was weak to begin with, weaker still and groggy from all the tranquilizers she'd taken. I just smothered her with a pillow on the couch, brought her back up here, took half the tranquilizers from the bottle, typed up a suicide note, and faked her signature. Simple enough.''

"Then knocked me out when I got here to check on her.''

Kurt nodded. "I'd overheard you say you were coming to check on her that night. I didn't want you to find her, didn't want anyone to see her until the police had time to find her confession and think the case was wrapped up.''

"You could have killed me that night.''

"Yes. But I decided having you just out of the way was better. I didn't know how much you figured out, how much Elsa might have already told you, who you might have talked to. So I wanted to see what you would do after Elsa was dead. Go on. What else have you figured out?''

"You hated Friedrich because he—not your father—killed your mother all those years ago. Or else he helped your father kill her. I'm not sure which, but I am sure he was instrumental in your mother's death.''

Kurt recoiled slightly, as if hearing the truth stated out loud made it even more horrifying, more enraging than it had been during all the dark, sleepless nights he had contemplated it.

"Yes. Yes. He killed my mother and, in a sense, my father, too. My father wouldn't have killed himself if he hadn't been in jail, if he hadn't lost his appeal. The Kauffmans kept me for a while, but then I was sent away. To homes. To people who didn't give a shit about me. My life has been one long mess—and I have Friedrich to thank for that.''

Softly Patricia said, "But there was one person who meant a lot to you. Jack Grierson."

Kurt closed his eyes for a second at the name, then opened them quickly. "Jack was my best friend in Vietnam. In my life. I watched him die in an explosion."

"Using his name—at the motel, to buy the hatpins—linked you to him. Your name was on a list of all the members of his command."

"That's how you figured out it was me?"

"That's how I connected you to the hatpins. I found the case against your father in a legal database of state court cases. That's when the pieces started fitting together. But not all of them."

Kurt's eyes narrowed on her.

"There are still some things I don't understand," Patricia said.

Kurt cocked the gun. Patricia's heart raced, her bowels and stomach clenched. It was hard to breathe evenly, but she forced herself to stay calm. She had to keep him talking, not just so she'd learn the truth, but so the police would have time to get here—if Brenda had followed her instructions. She had a backup plan just in case, but she didn't want to have to use it.

Patricia took a deep breath. "Come on, Kurt. You didn't just not kill me to see what I'd do. You wanted me, or someone, to figure this out. You want to tell someone the story. Why else use a name that links you directly to the murder? Why else use the hatpins to deliver the messages to Friedrich? If I dug hard enough, I'd find the connection, and I'd still connect you to the murder, even without using your buddy's name. If you'd just wanted Friedrich dead, you could have shot him or poisoned his coffee or something a little less obvious. But you wanted revenge, and to humiliate Friedrich, and what good is that without at least one person knowing the ugly truth about him?"

Kurt blinked hard. He was fighting back tears. Good, thought Patricia, maybe his emotions would put him off guard

. . . but then his expression became hard and cold. It wasn't going to be that easy.

Patricia swallowed. "Tell me about the hatpins."

Kurt frowned and looked away, as if he were looking at a different time, a different place. But he kept the gun trained steadily on Patricia. "I wanted Friedrich to remember. I wanted him to squirm, getting those, lie awake at night wondering who could know, who could have seen."

He looked at Patricia suddenly, sharply, anger puckering his face. "Elsa intercepted the notes. Protecting her father, as always. Someone was always protecting Friedrich, while he tore apart other people's lives. He never even saw them—never even realized—until the night I killed him.

"I had been away for years—just had a yearly Christmas card exchange with my Great-Aunt Gertrude. Then Elsa called, told me Gertrude had died, told me she had asked Elsa on her deathbed to let me know when she passed away, that she'd like me to come up for her funeral. So I came. I thought it might be nice to be around family again. I've spent most of my years alone, unable to get close to anyone."

Kurt laughed bitterly. "Ever since I lived with the Kauffman family, I wanted to fit in somewhere. I wanted to stay with them. They seemed so close to a little kid whose parents fought a lot. Of course, how could Friedrich stand to have me around? But he didn't know what I'd seen. And I'd forgotten it—suppressed it—until I saw those hatpins again."

Kurt pulled a handkerchief from his pocket, wiped his brow, and stuffed the handkerchief back in his pocket. The house was not that warm, but he was sweating, and his hands were starting to shake.

"Anyway, I saw the hatpins at the auction of Great-Aunt Gertrude's things, and it came back to me. That night, I'd heard noises—my mother's voice, Friedrich's. They were loud. I was scared; I got up and went to my parents' bedroom and looked in. Friedrich was kissing my mom. She was at her dressing table, and he was bent over her. I was too young to understand entirely, but knew something was wrong—he shouldn't have been in there with her. My mom pushed him away and laughed. I'll never forget that now—her tilting her head back, laughing at him. Suddenly he slapped her. She stood up, her nose bleeding. She started to hit him, but he grabbed her arm. And then he grabbed a hatpin from the dressing table. And stabbed her in the throat and chest— again and again.

"The police talked to me later that night—wanted to know if I'd seen or heard anything. I told them no, I'd slept through the night until they woke me up. And it was true—it was what I believed, until I saw the hatpins at the auction again, and it all came back to me."

Kurt sat very still, his eyes on Patricia but focused else- where. He was seeing the scene again that he had seen as a little boy. Patricia wondered how many times he'd replayed it, over and over, into the sleepless nights, and into restless dreams, as he'd plotted his revenge.

"And then you bought the hatpins from the antique dealer in Lebanon," Patricia said.

"Yes. It was impulse. I saw the woman buy them, found out later that day who it was, then went up to Lebanon and bought the whole lot myself. Using Jack's name in that damned register was just impulse at the time. I wasn't think- ing clearly, not sure what to do. I just got the hatpins and went back to Florida. And that's where I started piecing things together."

Kurt's eyes narrowed. "You know what that bastard told me? You know what Friedrich said the night I confronted him? He told me he and my mother had been lovers. She told him she wanted money, enough to get away from me and my father, or she'd say he raped her, ruin him. He killed her in anger, grabbing a hatpin Gertrude had given her. He told me that like it should let him off the hook." Kurt paused, bit his lip. "That's when I hit him, knocked him into the table. And then I stabbed him with the hatpin I'd kept for the purpose, again and again just like he did my mother."

"While you were in Florida, you came up with your plan for revenge," Patricia said. Keep him talking, she thought, keep him on the story. She needed to keep buying time and pray that Brenda had done as she asked.

"Yes. It was so simple. I just moved back here, buddied up again with the Kauffman family, got to know Friedrich's habits, when he was alone. Friedrich was happy enough to accept me in his firm—guilt, I guess. Even a shit like him could have guilt. And of course he didn't know then what I'd witnessed. Then I said I was going to Florida for vacation. Had Elsa make the reservations, paid for them and everything.

"But instead I hitchhiked to just south of Cincinnati, to the Blue Bird Motel, where I'd also made reservations using Jack's name. Kept myself disguised and away from people. I used a pay phone at the diner to call down to the Florida motel to check on any messages. Got a ride with a trucker back up to Cincinnati two different nights, with a carful of teenagers another night."

"And things were going fine until somehow Andy got in the way?" Patricia asked.

"Yes. He came by one night while I was at the office to leave one of the hatpin notes. He was immediately suspicious, of course. He'd been trying to catch me at the Florida motel over a client; I'd called him back once. When he saw me, he was ready to cause trouble. But I knew him. He was a greedy one—the only thing that talked to him was money. So I convinced him to drive back down to Kentucky with me, told him I had a scam going to get a lot of money out of Friedrich and I'd cut him in if he came with me."

Patricia nodded. "From what I learned of his background, he'd fall for that."

"Yeah, he was really eager. He wanted to drive down, and I said fine, but we had to park on the outskirts of town, leave his car out in the countryside. I told him we had to be really careful, secretive. I got him in the motel room, knocked him out, tied him up. Then I strangled him. I stayed one more night. Then I took his car—I was careful later to clean my fingerprints off the steering wheel and door handle—and went back up to Cincinnati. I left the car parked on a street near Andy's apartment.

"Then I just lived in the streets, spent a few nights at a homeless shelter. I didn't want anyone to see me at my apartment, since I had told my landlord and everyone else I'd be in Florida. I watched for Friedrich to work late. I didn't have to wait long. He came back after hours by himself one night. A few days after I killed him, I called my motel in Florida from a pay phone and found I had a message from Elsa. I called her, and she told me that her father had been killed, and so had Andy. I told her I'd rush right home."

"There's a point I don't quite understand, Kurt. . . ."

Kurt shook his head. He'd had his momentary fill of the past, of his bitterness, she realized. She couldn't get him to relive more of his past to buy the time she needed. "No more questions, Patricia. You got the story you wanted."

"You can kill me, Kurt. But others will figure this out. Things haven't gone as smoothly as you've planned. Elsa and Andy got in your way, now me." Kurt frowned, looking uncomfortable. "The more people you kill, the more people will ask questions. Sooner or later you'll get caught. If you turn yourself in now . . ."

Kurt shook his head vehemently. "My father died in jail. I'll die before I go there. Sorry, Patricia, but I'm going to take my chances with killing you. And whoever else I have to." He cleared his throat. "Stand up."

Patricia sat very still. Brenda, apparently, had fallen through on plan A. It was time for plan B.

"Stand up, goddammit!"

Patricia jumped from her chair suddenly, throwing the album at him, and dived behind the bed. Kurt fired off two shots. One bullet went into a wall. Another grazed her leg. She breathed evenly, pushing down the sudden pain, the desire to scream, and focused on the afghan on the end of the bed. Dean's gun from the tavern was in it, hidden in the middle fold. She had slipped it in there as soon as she came in the room, in case Kurt decided to frisk her, and had hoped she could stay close to it.

Kurt was stepping toward her.

She slipped her hand into the fold of the afghan, pulled out the gun just as Kurt came around the corner of the bed.

Patricia pulled the trigger of the nine-millimeter semi-automatic. She closed her eyes and kept pulling the trigger, firing off one shot after another.

When there was silence, finally, she opened her eyes. Her shoulder was throbbing in agonizing pain. Kurt had gotten one more shot into her. And then she saw him. He was sprawled on the floor, a bloody mess. Three bullets had gone into his face and chest, the rest into the bedroom wall.

Patricia looked away and fought back throwing up. She calmed herself down enough to get on the bed and collapse. She wrapped the afghan around her shoulder. Then, at last, she heard the police pulling in the driveway, doors slamming. She forced herself up off the bed and went to meet them.

Chapter 25

Patricia leaned back in her chair and smiled with satisfaction at the computer screen. She had finished writing up her report for Alliston College on Dr. Hauser, the professorial candidate who, she discovered, had plagiarized his dissertation and, as it turned out, had been accused at his last position of soliciting sexual favors from two young girls in one of his classes. Patricia couldn't really say in her business that she always had happy customers—truth served itself, not happiness or any other emotion—but Alliston College would be glad to have the information and avoid the mistake of hiring Hauser.

She heard three quick knocks, and then her door opening.

"Hi, Dean," she said without looking up.

"How do you know it's me?"

"Because you're the only one who has the nerve to enter my office without being asked." Except for Henry Kauffman a few weeks ago, Patricia remembered.

"I knocked!"

"Three times, like always."

"My habits are giving me away."

Dean opened the mini-blind to the window, filling the dim room suddenly with bright sunlight. Dean settled into a visitor's chair and put a bag on the desk. Patricia could smell submarine sandwiches in the bag, and they made her stomach growl. She kept looking at the computer, though, wanting to finish proofreading the report.

"Hey, are you going to have lunch with me or what? You're

the one who called whining about a sudden desire for Al's Best Subs.''

"I know, I know. Just a second—''

"Where's the plug on this little gray box—''

"Okay! Hold on. Just let me finish reading this last sentence . . . and save this file.'' Patricia tapped a few keys then looked up at Dean. "Ta-da. I'm done.''

Dean grinned. He opened the bag and got out two submarine sandwiches, ham with extra provolone for him, turkey and salami for Patricia, and plenty of banana peppers, lettuce, tomato, and mayonnaise on both. He got out two cups of Coke, too.

Patricia bit into her sub, consumed the bite ravenously, and took another. "Yum.''

"Is this the first time you've looked up from that box of yours all day?''

"Um, yeah.'' She took another big bite. "Why?''

"You've been blinking like a mole since I opened the mini-blind.''

"Thanks.''

A few minutes later Patricia finished the sub. She wadded up the sandwich wrapper, tossed it back into the bag, and took a long drink of Coke.

"Wow. Did you eat that, or inhale it?'' Dean still had a third of his sub left.

"Us moles get really hungry.''

Dean put the remainder of his sub down. "I'm glad to see you hungry. You must be feeling better.''

Patricia nodded. "I'm doing all right. Shoulder's still stiff. Doc says that may take a while to go away.''

"A slug in the shoulder—that's pretty serious stuff.''

"I know.''

"You're damned lucky.''

"I know,'' she said quietly. She looked away from Dean, not able to face the concern in his eyes. She opened a drawer, got out his gun, and slid it across the table to him.

"Police finally gave it back,'' she said. "Thanks.''

Dean just stared at it, then looked up at her, his expression now a mix of anger and concern. "If I'd have known what you were up to—"

"I told you I was going on a dangerous stakeout. That's what it was, kind of. We've been over this before."

"Yeah. And I still don't know why you had to go face-to-face with someone you knew was a killer."

Patricia looked at the gray screen of her computer, the only activity on it now a blinking cursor next to the first option on the menu of word processing, spread sheets, and databases she'd set up. It was waiting for her next command.

"I wanted to get at the truth myself. I didn't know if the police would believe me enough to find out for themselves, or if I'd ever learn the truth if they did. I wanted the truth."

How many times had she warned her clients that the truth could be dangerous? Now, however, she better understood their need to pursue its perils.

Patricia looked back at Dean. "That's it. My motive."

Dean shook his head. He picked up the gun, looked at it. "This had never been fired before."

"I'd never killed anyone before," Patricia said quietly.

"It bothers you."

She shrugged. "I did what I had to do. I wanted to live."

"I know you better than that, Patricia. It bothers you."

She half smiled. "I'll deal with it." She had been meditating a lot lately. And for the past few days, despite her doctor's orders, playing the drums, hard. Extra hard. It strained and pulled her shoulder, making the injury burn all over again, but somehow that helped her more than anything, feeling the slow burn in her shoulder.

The phone rang.

"I'd better get this," Patricia said.

Dean picked up his sandwich and continued eating as she answered the phone.

"Patricia Delaney, investigative consultant."

"You can cut the formality, Patty-cakes," the voice screeched on the other end. "It's Sis."

Patricia sighed. "Maureen. How about a 'how are you? Gee, I'm glad you're alive.' "

"Sure I'm glad. You've got to call Lucy!"

"Lucy? What's wrong with her? She was okay when I talked with her last night."

"So. You've been talking with her." Maureen's voice was cold and distant now, stony with hurt and a sense of betrayal.

"Yeah, I talked with her."

"Well, talk with her again! I've got to get her away from Mom and Dad. I need her back here with me."

"Why, Maureen?"

"Why? Why? 'Cause I'm alone, that's why! I need Lucy back with me. She needs to be back with me."

"She needs to find her own way in the world, that's what she needs," Patricia said.

"By going off to be an artist next year? I listened to you, and look at my life. Now you're doing the same thing to Lucy! You can't—"

Patricia sat up straight in her chair. "Let's get something straight, Maureen. Maybe I should have kept my mouth shut years ago. But I didn't. I also didn't force you to live the way you have, or to make the choices you have. And neither has Lucy. As for her, she'll make her own choices, and they'll probably be pretty good ones for her, because she'll have made them for herself. You might want to think about doing the same for yourself, Maureen. Get on with living."

Maureen was crying. "You don't understand—you—"

Patricia sighed. Maureen didn't know what Patricia meant, and she probably never would. "I understand too well, Maureen. And I have to go. We'll talk some other time when you're calmer." She put the telephone receiver down gently.

"What was all that about?"

Patricia half smiled, straightened a stack of invoices on her desk. "Closing up another case. A personal one."

"I should know better than to ask too many questions."

"Yes."

"Here's one, though. There's a party this weekend—"

Patricia shook her head before Dean could finish. "Some other time Dean, I'd love to. Really would. I'm going camping this weekend."

"By yourself?"

Patricia laughed at Dean's little-boy pout of jealousy. "By myself, I promise. Look—I just need a little time alone to think. Sort some stuff out in my head."

Dean nodded. "I understand." He tossed his sandwich wrapper back in the bag. Then he picked up the gun and stuck it in the bag, too. "I guess I'll carry the gun out in this. Don't want to scare your fellow tenants."

He started to the door.

"Dean?"

He turned and faced Patricia. "Yeah?"

"Thanks for—everything."

"No sweat, Patricia."

"Dean?"

"Yeah, Patricia?"

"Want to—want to go to a movie next week?"

Dean smiled. "Sure. Call me when you're back from camping."

She nodded. "I will."

Dean left. For a second Patricia looked at the closed door. Then she sat back down, knowing she ought to get back to work. She had only been back to work for a week, and she had a backlog of clients and cases to attend to.

The Kauffman cases were, finally, closed. Kurt had confessed the truth. Leroy Hibberd, once Patricia gave all the information she had about him to the police, admitted that he had always suspected Friedrich's involvement with Wilma Knepper's murder, although he had never known for certain that Friedrich had killed her. Russell, always jealous and suspicious, had hired Leroy to stake out his house when he was away at night. Sure enough, Friedrich was a frequent visitor, and he had photos to prove it. He also had photos showing Friedrich coming out of the house early one morning, blood on his shirt, running for the car. Russell had used the photos to blackmail Friedrich all these years, keeping several copies of them in various safe-deposit boxes, and instructions with his wife and attorney on where to find them in case of his death, just in case Friedrich decided to take the easy way out of blackmail payments.

Patricia had not told Henry what she learned about Brenda and Tom, but Brenda had. She made a deal with Henry to give up her claim in the family business for now and always, in exchange for keeping the $100,000 and not being prosecuted for taking it. At lunch with Patricia, Brenda had seemed satisfied and happy with the arrangement, eager to get out on her own and prove that she could operate independently. She was going to build her own business, starting with the investment she had made outside of Columbus. When Patricia asked about Tom, Brenda just smiled. Tom was on his own again, free to make his fortune or not, but without Brenda's help.

The case was satisfactorily wrapped up, but Patricia was still haunted by the knowledge that Elsa had confronted Kurt on her own, wanting to be like the image she had of Patricia as brave and strong.

Brave, Patricia thought. She wasn't sure she could honestly describe herself as brave. She had put herself in a dangerous situation out of anger and a need for some answers, but that was not the same thing as being brave.

She thought that Elsa, supposedly the weak one of the Kauffman family, had, at the end, understood bravery more than any of them. Her bravery did not lie in her final foolish act of facing Kurt; she should have gone to the police immediately with what she knew. But Elsa had realized the truth, and she had not used it to manipulate others, as Leroy Hibberd had, or hidden from it, as Friedrich had, or used it as an excuse for her own failings, as Kurt had. She had simply understood it, and faced it in the best way she knew how.

Patricia swiveled in her chair and looked at the new picture on the wall over her desk. It was the sketch Lucy had drawn of her and Sammie by the edge of the woods. She smiled to herself and started shutting up the office. Her Chevy S-10 was already packed with camping gear for the weekend, and she knew just the place she wanted to go.

She was quitting work earlier than she ever had before on

a Friday afternoon, but further business could wait until Monday. It was time for the trek in the woods the sketch had made her dream about, where she walked with Sammie at her side, finally at peace with the events of the past weeks, finally regaining peace with herself.